Caddie si̲
wouldn't thi̲

The captain had trusted her enough to send her out with a detail of six men. She would forget about the boatswain's perpetual scowl and his antipathy to female petty officers.

Maybe after a while, when she wasn't so benumbed, she'd roll over on her side. She couldn't lie on her left side because of her broken arm and the lump on her temple. She'd have to try her right side. Later.

What would her mother say? Her eyelids flew open and she winced. Mom would have fits. Caddie's first long deployment in Alaskan waters, and she'd been injured. Smail seemed to think she'd get several weeks of medical leave. She'd like to go home for a visit, though Mom would fuss over her. Would that be so bad? And would the Coast Guard pay for her flight? Probably not. Of course, if she left Kodiak, she wouldn't see Aven Holland again.

That was a depressing thought. She'd only met the *Milroy's* boatswain's mate once—at church a few weeks ago—but she'd hoped to see him again soon. Whenever they were both in port again. Which could be tricky when they served on different ships.

But that's good, she sleepily reminded herself. If they were on the same ship, they wouldn't be allowed to date. But since she was on the *Wintergreen* and Aven was on the *Milroy*, they might actually have a chance. . . .

She drifted off into blessed velvety darkness.

SUSAN PAGE DAVIS and her husband, Jim, have been married thirty-three years and have six children, ages fourteen to thirty-one. They live in Maine, where they are active in an independent Baptist church. Susan is a homeschooling mother and writes historical romance, mystery, and suspense novels. Visit her Web site at: www.susanpagedavis.com.

Books by Susan Page Davis

HEARTSONG PRESENTS
HP607—Protecting Amy
HP692—Oregon Escort
HP708—The Prisoner's Wife
HP719—Weaving a Future
HP727—Wyoming Hoofbeats
HP739—The Castaway's Bride
HP756—The Lumberjack's Lady
HP800—Return to Love
HP811—A New Joy
HP827—Abiding Peace
HP850—Trail to Justice

Always Ready

Susan Page Davis

Heartsong Presents

To all our military men and women, especially Michael. Thank you for all you're doing and have done.

Acknowledgements:
A great many people helped me research and write this book, including: LuAnn and Dana Nordine; Aven Leidigh; Henry Kurgan of Homer by the Sea; pilot Kelly Leseman; Captain David MacKenzie, USCG (ret.); CWO Scott MacAloon, USCG; CWO-3 Peter J. Davenport, USCG; CWO-3 Gilman C. Page, USCG (ret.); Darlene Franklin; Lynette Sowell; James S. Davis. Thank you all!

A note from the Author:
I love to hear from my readers! You may correspond with me by writing:

Susan Page Davis
Author Relations
PO Box 721
Uhrichsville, OH 44683

ISBN 978-1-60260-575-6

ALWAYS READY

Our mission is to publish and distribute inspirational products offering exceptional value and biblical encouragement to the masses.

PRINTED IN THE U.S.A.

one

Caddie Lyle stood on the bridge of the ship, watching out the windows ahead as the farthest Aleutian Islands came into view. The crew of her ship, the U.S. Coast Guard's buoy tender *Wintergreen*, was carrying out its early summer assignment to check their most remote navigational aids and deliver supplies to a few isolated Native Alaskan villages. Volcanic mountains formed an eerily beautiful backdrop to the frothing seascape that stretched before them into infinity. The 225-foot ship seemed a tiny bit of flotsam.

The Bering Sea writhed all around the ship, tossing it up and down in nauseating plunges. Caddie braced her feet as a particularly violent lurch hit the ship and focused on a large map hanging on the wall across the room. Seasickness rarely overtook her, but she'd struggled the past forty-eight hours in the inhospitable waters of the North.

The skipper paused beside her and looked forward out the big windows at the barely visible land in the distance. "In a few hours, we'll be at the western end of the USA."

Caddie nodded and pulled in a deep breath. Her stomach settled down as the deck found a more level plane. "Can't believe I'm really out here."

"You can believe it. We'll put in at Attu soon. When our errand there's completed, we'll head on home."

Home and family seemed worlds away. Of all the people Caddie loved, only her father had seen these waters. Like her, he had come years ago with supplies for the Coast Guard station at Attu, the last in the chain of Aleutian islands.

She stared out the side windows, where nothing but waves and sky existed. This wild setting reduced the massive *Wintergreen* to a fragile bark. But God was still above, keeping them afloat. She smiled at the thought.

"Sir," Lindsey Rockwell, their operations specialist, called to the captain from her post at the radio desk, "I'm getting a distress signal."

The skipper hurried to her side. "What type of vessel?"

"It's a Russian trawler. We're the nearest ship, although they may be just outside our jurisdiction."

"Let's go. What's their position?"

Caddie dashed to the desk where she worked when plotting the ship's course. As the captain gave the orders for a change of direction, she entered the new course on her computer console then carefully wrote it in the log.

In less than an hour, during which Lindsey maintained contact with the Russian ship's crew, the trawler appeared on the horizon. As they drew closer, Caddie could see that the fishing boat sat very low in the choppy water, sluggishly riding each wave and turning willy-nilly with the elements. She wished she had her camera but couldn't leave the bridge to fetch it from the tiny cabin she shared with Lindsey.

"Crew of fourteen in a small boat," Lindsey called out. "The skipper is now leaving the trawler, and he's the last man off."

"Where are they?" The captain searched the heaving surface with his binoculars.

"I've lost contact, but I assume they're pulling away from the trawler."

"Well, that thing's going under before we can reach it." Captain Raven shook his head.

Every man on the bridge scurried for binoculars. All was silent for several seconds as they scanned the water around the trawler.

Caddie prayed the fishermen could get far enough from

their doomed boat that they wouldn't be capsized by the waves it made when it sank.

A shout came from outside. "Lookout reports the vessel on the horizon, sir," Lindsey said. "Small boat at two-eight-zero."

"There!" The captain pointed. "Alter course."

As the crew rushed to obey, he whirled toward Caddie. "Get down on the main deck, Lyle. I'll give you half a dozen hands to help get those Russians on board. You oversee the operation."

"Aye, aye, sir." Caddie turned and ran for the ladder, hearing the captain's voice echo over the loudspeaker. When she hit the bottom stair, seamen were already streaming onto the buoy deck. She rattled off orders to prepare to lower a workboat over the side to assist the Russians.

The small boat was swung out and lowered until it was even with the rail. She and the men grabbed lifejackets. The deck crew scurried to man the falls that would lower the workboat.

Caddie hastily fastened her bright yellow life vest. She tried not to think too hard about the job ahead. Nerves wouldn't help her now. The boatswain was surely watching her from the forecastle windows above, but she avoided looking up there. She kept her eyes on either the Russian trawler or the men assigned to her. Boatswain Tilley always set her adrenaline pumping with his critical frown. Even when she did well, she sensed that he didn't completely approve of her.

The *Wintergreen* drew nearer to the small boat in which the fishing crew had escaped. It was little more than a rowboat, tossing on the violent waves. A dozen men huddled inside it, while two more clung to the gunwales, their bodies in the icy water. They'd never make it without help.

Caddie and her crew boarded the workboat and she radioed the bridge. "Boat crew is ready."

"Affirmative."

The deck crew lowered the workboat with her and the crew inside. It hit the water perfectly, on the crest of a wave, and she gave a mental cheer for the men manning the apparatus. She nodded for Jackson to start the motor, and they cut across the mammoth waves toward the Russians. Leaving the side of the *Wintergreen*, they caught the full force of the wind and rolling seas. She grabbed the gunwale beside her as a huge sweep of water caught them and heaved them skyward.

Lord, get us through this!

As they rushed down into the trough between waves, the thought that she and her crew might end up needing rescue flitted through her mind, but soon they were close enough to the Russian boat that her helmsman cut the engine so they could approach with caution. Two of the fishermen were leaning over the side of their craft, trying to haul another man aboard. Their boat tipped precariously. Caddie prayed that she could reach the men in time.

She radioed back to the ship, "*Wintergreen*, this is *Wintergreen 1*. We're approaching small boat to give assistance."

One of her seaman apprentices yelled, and she looked where he pointed. The beleaguered trawler's prow had tilted upward, and with the next large wave, it sank from sight. The Russians who saw it paused in their labor for a moment, staring back toward the empty sea where their ship had been. The two trying to help the man in the water seemed oblivious.

As Caddie turned her attention back to their small boat, a giant wave caught the little craft broadside and tilted the hull, spilling several of the fishermen into the water on the other side.

She yelled into the wind, "Hurry!"

Jackson nodded and moved the throttle, sending them

between two flailing Russians. One of them swam toward the Coast Guard boat and caught hold of the side. Two seamen hurried to assist him. On the other side of the boat, the fisherman in the water thrashed and sank below the surface. His head bobbed up again, and one of Caddie's men tossed out a life preserver tied to a line. The man lunged at it and hung on as the seaman pulled him in.

Caddie assessed the situation. The Russian lifeboat was still afloat, though it had taken on a lot of water. She counted seven men in it. Two in the water held to the sides, though she wasn't sure they were the same two who had clung to it earlier. Another man floated between her and the other boat, and beyond it, a nearly submerged fisherman waved frantically.

With two Russians now in her boat, Caddie gestured to Jackson, urging him to approach the nearest swimmer. In less than two minutes, they had another coughing, shivering man aboard. A seaman's apprentice distributed blankets and extra life vests to those who needed them.

They were close to the little boat now. It was only half the length of the Coast Guard workboat. Caddie cupped her hands and screamed to one of the men in it, "Are you okay?"

He looked blankly at her and pointed to the man in the water on his side of the boat. Caddie looked beyond to the man fifty yards out on the other side. That man didn't stand a chance, whereas the two clinging to the boat might last a few minutes while the Coast Guard helped their comrade. It was a judgment call, and she couldn't waste time agonizing over it. She threw the Russian in the boat a lifejacket—their last extra—and waved Jackson to head for the swimmer beyond.

When she looked back, the Russian was leaning over to help the man in the water pull the lifejacket on. If they couldn't hoist him into their boat, at least he'd float until she returned. On the other side, more Russian fishermen succeeded in lifting the other man who had clung to the gunwales at the side into the boat and comparative safety.

Jackson skillfully judged the waves and brought the workboat close to the swimmer. Caddie stared in disbelief. The bearded Russian held another man's head barely above the surface of the water. Jackson turned the boat and edged in closer. Caddie and the three Russians they'd rescued balanced the weight of the seamen as they leaned over to grab the inert man first.

As soon as they pulled the body away from him, the swimmer sank, thrashing his arms.

"No!" Caddie screamed. Jackson puttered close to where he'd gone down and swung the boat sideways.

Afraid they'd run over him, Caddie leaned over to peer into the water. A wave lifted them and drenched her. She fell back into the boat. How would they ever find him again? Was he already drifting to the bottom?

When the boat stabilized once more, she grabbed a life preserver and stood amidships, testing her balance as she swung the life ring back and forth. A moment later she tossed it out over the waves. Not until it landed with a splash did she see the fisherman's head. The man reached, fell short, rallied, and tried again. Once more, he failed to catch the life ring.

Awkward movements to her left caught her eye. Seaman Gavin, in the bow of her boat, had clipped a line to his life vest and handed the coil to another man. Now he stooped and was removing his boots. Before Caddie could protest, he dove over the side and swam toward the Russian.

Her heart leaped into her throat as she watched his progress. Even though Gavin wore the lifejacket, he wouldn't be able to survive in this rough, icy water for long.

As the Russian man began to sink again, Gavin reached him and yanked him to the surface by his hair. The man dove toward Gavin, overwhelming him in an embrace that carried both beneath the surface.

"Pull them in," Caddie yelled. Three seamen jumped to obey.

Already, Gavin had popped up again and managed to turn the weakened Russian to a towing position. In minutes the two were in the boat.

Again Caddie evaluated their situation. They now had five Russians aboard, and the fishermen's boat held eight. Had they lost one? She looked all around, searching the waves. The Russians had four oars in the water and attempted to row toward the towering side of the *Wintergreen*.

Caddie cupped her hands and yelled at them, but the wind caught her words. One of the Russians saw her and raised his hand. Caddie shouted, "Five!" She held her gloved hand high, fingers outspread and then pointed into the bottom of her boat. "Five men!"

The Russian frowned then nodded. He jostled the man next to him and spoke to him.

"Should we head in?" Jackson yelled.

She swung around and scanned the sea again. There had to be one more man. When she looked back toward the Russians, their boat had reached the lee of the *Wintergreen* and huddled against the ship. Coastguardsmen above yelled instructions down at them, and one of the Russians reached for the ladder he could climb to safety.

Caddie pulled out her radio. "*Wintergreen*, this is *Wintergreen 1*. I have five Russian fishermen in my boat. Request you get a count on the passengers in their boat. There should be fourteen total."

During the pause that followed, she looked over the drenched men shivering in her boat. They shook with cold, despite the blankets. One man lay on the deck with his eyes closed, his lips blue. Caddie watched his chest for a long moment, terrified until it rose with his gasp for breath.

Gavin also trembled uncontrollably. Several of her other men were soaked through and hugging themselves for warmth. They all stared at her, waiting for her order.

"*Wintergreen 1,* we've got eight Russians. Over," came the captain's voice over her radio.

Caddie's heart sank. "Any sign of another man in the water? Over."

"Negative. We've been looking. We thought you'd got the last one."

She inhaled deeply. "Await your instructions, sir. Over."

"Come aboard, Lyle."

"Aye, aye, sir. We're en route to the *Wintergreen.* Our ETA is five minutes." She nodded to Jackson. "Return to the ship."

The last of the eight Russians from the rowboat was climbing the ladder as Caddie's boat approached the ship. The now-empty, fifteen-foot wooden boat was tied to the ladder and bounced as each wave hit it. It swung around and crashed into the ship's hull.

"Careful!" Caddie turned to tell Jackson to ease in and let one of the other men latch onto the empty boat. They would have to move it out of the way and position the workboat beneath the davits to be lifted.

Just beyond them a giant wave towered. "Hold on!" she screamed and groped for a firm grip on the gunwale.

The wave hit them with a shock that pulled loose her grasp and threw her against the thwart. Air rushed out of her lungs. Icy water engulfed her for a few seconds. Amid the yelling and thrashing of the men, cold and weakness overwhelmed her. Then came excruciating pain.

❧

Boatswain's mate Aven Holland picked his way among a horde of huge salmon, across the slippery deck of the fishing boat *Molly K.* The skipper, Jason Andrews, who fished out of

Seward, had crossed his path before. He operated his boat just within the boundaries of safety and commercial fishing regulations. Aven determined to check every detail today.

Two of his crew of four seamen climbed up the ladder from the fishing boat's hold and crossed the deck to where he stood near the boat's owner. Aven took a few steps to meet them.

Seaman Kusiak kept his voice low and glanced past Aven, then back into his eyes. "Sir, their weight is off."

"Don't call me sir."

"Sorry. But it is."

"You sure?" Aven asked.

"Yes, s—Yes."

"How much?"

"Five hundred pounds, give or take."

Aven whistled softly. "I'll come down. We don't want to make any mistakes."

Kusiak's shoulders relaxed. "Right."

Aven said to the second man, "Wayne, you stay up here with the skipper. Don't take any guff from him."

As he headed for the ladder, Aven called his commanding officer on his handheld radio. The law enforcement cutter stood off a quarter mile, waiting while three teams conducted inspections on fishing vessels.

Aven wished he'd gone to check another boat. But no, he'd asked for this one. Did he want to cross swords with Andrews again? He didn't like to think he was spoiling for a fight. Last time he'd let Andrews by with a warning on a minor violation and regretted it. Did he secretly hope for a rematch and a chance to catch the fisherman breaking the law? Aven had nothing to prove. Maybe he should have let the other boatswain's mate take this boat and avoided the confrontation with a man who already disliked him.

When the operations officer on the bridge of the *Milroy*

answered his call, Aven said, "We have a weight discrepancy and will be issuing a citation."

He climbed quickly but carefully down into the work area in the lower part of the fishing boat. The deck below lay ankle-deep in fish, mostly big salmon. Refrigerated lockers on both sides bulged with thousands of pounds of fish. The footing was slimy and treacherous, the stench overpowering. Aven gritted his teeth. At least he was in charge of the detail now, but it seemed he would still end up weighing, measuring, and counting fish, the same as his men had been doing all day. He might never want to eat salmon again.

Two more seamen, wearing jackets and gloves in the refrigerated area, continued the inspection process of weighing, measuring, and recording. They probed into all the recesses of the ship to be sure they'd seen everything. Sometimes fishermen pulled in a catch and threw overboard the lower-grade fish they'd snagged, keeping only the top grade. The only way to prove this illegal and wasteful practice was catching the fishermen in the act. Or they might accidentally catch protected species. Apparently this crew hadn't tried to keep any illegal bycatch.

Checking the amount of fish in the hold against the numbers in the fishermen's records was tedious but doable. Aven spent more time doing this than anything else during Alaska's fishing seasons. The crew of his law enforcement cutter made sure commercial fisheries didn't harvest more than the law allowed from Alaskan waters.

The *Milroy* had been out a week from Kodiak, plying the most popular fishing shoals. The cutter's appearance in a new location this morning had no doubt made a lot of fishermen uneasy.

As soon as today's work ended and all hands were back aboard the *Milroy*, the cutter would head back to Kodiak. The quick thought of his home base brought an eager longing. Aven had been at this for eight years now, the last four in his home state's frigid waters. He didn't mind a cruise on the roiling, icy sea, but the hassle he got from fishermen who broke the law made the job less attractive. Still, it was worth being close enough to home that he could get to Wasilla to see his family several times a year.

Right now the fatigue of fisheries law enforcement had worn him down. He'd be glad to get back to Kodiak Island and spend some time on land. Maybe he'd even make it to church this Sunday.

Church. Would the buoy tender *Wintergreen* be in port now? If so, the new boatswain's mate third class would probably be at church Sunday morning. He'd met her there a few weeks ago, before her ship put out for an extended deployment. Caddie Lyle. He could picture her serious blue eyes and pert nose. She wasn't beautiful, but she had a wholesome attractiveness and a quiet determination that appealed to him. The memory of her perked him up considerably as they weighed the slippery, smelly fish. Next time they were both in port, he would ask her out. That settled, he got on with the job.

An hour in the cold storage unit was unpleasant, but it gave him enough time to double-check the seamen's weigh-ins. Time to issue the citation to the boat's captain. Meanwhile, he assigned another man to run through the checklist of safety requirements.

He emerged smelly and sticky into the fresh air on deck again, convinced his men's assessment was accurate. He pulled in a deep breath. It was summer in Alaska, but the sea air still held an arctic edge, and the waters remained icy cold. If a man fell over the side, the frigid waves would sap his strength in seconds, and his heavy clothing would drag him down.

On the main deck, Wayne still stood a few feet from

Andrews, who looked none too happy. The rest of the boat's crew had stopped working and milled aimlessly about the deck, waiting for Aven's verdict. Adjusting his gait to the rolling of the boat, he walked over and handed the skipper his clipboard and showed him where to sign the inspection form.

"I can't talk you out of this?" the bearded man growled.

"No, sir. You can appeal if you wish, but we've verified the discrepancies in weight twice. You're carrying way more salmon than your records claim."

"Your scales disagree with mine."

Aven shrugged. "Ours were calibrated three weeks ago, and they're the official instruments. If you were off by a few pounds, we wouldn't think much of it." He turned to Seaman Kusiak. "Did you check on mandatory safety equipment yet?"

Kusiak nodded. "Yes. They've got most of what's required." He held out a form.

Aven looked over the checklist and noted the lack of two personal flotation devices and a case of flares whose expiration date had come and gone. The captain would face a stiff fine for certain because of the bulging refrigeration lockers below. The safety violations would add more fines and red flag the boat for another inspection soon.

Aven beckoned Wayne a few steps away, down the deck, and asked quietly, "Anything else I should know?"

"Just that they're not happy."

"They never are. Did they threaten you while I was below?"

Wayne hesitated.

"Come on." Aven walked several paces away and turned around so that he faced the captain and crew but Wayne had his back to them.

"The big guy in the red hat."

Aven scanned the crewmen and nodded.

"He said something to the skipper about how easy it would be to get the jump on us."

"What did Andrews say?"

"Said he was nuts. The Guard would be all over them like a flock of seagulls on a garbage dump."

"He's right. Anything else?"

"No, just muttering and dirty looks."

"Okay. You and Kusiak be ready to get down into the boat. We'll board in a minute." Aven strode back to the captain and met his gaze for a long moment. "Make sure you've got all your PFDs next time." He tore off the carbon and handed Andrews the citation. "You'll be notified soon when and where to appear in court."

"Yeah, right." The captain squinted at the paper. The wind fluttered it, and he reached up with his other hand to hold it steady. Half a dozen of his crewmen closed in around him, glaring at Aven and his team. The hulking man in the red knit cap looked over the captain's shoulder at the paper and swore.

Aven did a quick mental assessment. When a man's livelihood and that of his whole crew was threatened, anything could happen. The Coastguardsmen were outnumbered. Although he had a pistol, his men were unarmed. No telling what weapons the fishermen carried. Prudence dictated that they make their exit.

"Thank you, gentlemen," he said.

"Just get off my boat." Andrews glared at him.

The big fisherman spat out a filthy insult, advancing a menacing step toward him.

Aven held his gaze. "I'd advise you to stay calm. I have the power to arrest you."

Three other men fell in beside the big man. One of them held a hooked fish gaff.

Aven reached for the button on his radio. The big man

swung fast—faster than Aven could react. The blow to his midsection sent him sprawling backward toward the rail where his men waited.

two

Caddie lay on the bunk in sick bay and focused on the lights overhead. The painkillers were already taking effect. The stabbing pangs in her arm had eased, but she still felt the deep, throbbing ache.

Edward Smail, the hospital corpsman who'd dressed her fractured arm, hovered over her. "All right, that should keep your arm immobilized until we get home and a real doctor can look at it. Let me look at that bump on your head now."

Caddie blinked in surprise, but when she'd absorbed his words, she realized that her head *did* ache, too. She put her right hand up to her hairline and carefully fingered the lump.

"I didn't even know I'd hit my head."

Smail shrugged. "That arm's going to give you something to think about for at least six weeks. But you've got a goose egg, too."

"Can I go to my quarters?"

"No, I think I'd better keep you here where I can observe you until we reach Kodiak." He smoothed her hair back and pulled in an overhead lamp on an expanding arm. "Yeah, that's a good one."

"Concussion?" she asked.

"Maybe. I'm not a doctor, but the men did say you were pretty groggy for a while. Didn't pass out completely, but disoriented for sure when I first laid eyes on you."

She scrunched up her face, but that hurt, so she forced herself to relax. "We lost a man."

"What?"

"One of the Russians. There were fourteen on board, and

19

we only got thirteen out of the water."

"I don't know about that. But I do know you did a good job."

She wasn't so sure. One man had died. How could anyone perceive that as acceptable?

The boatswain hadn't. She remembered strong hands lifting her to the deck of the *Wintergreen*, where the seamen had crowded around her. Distinctly, she'd heard Tilley mutter, "This is why men should take the hazardous duty."

"Can I sleep?" she asked. "I feel really tired."

Smail hesitated. "Okay, but I'll wake you up now and then to take your vitals and make sure you're still coherent."

She smiled wryly at that. "Right. I'm sure you've got a manual six inches thick to tell you exactly what to watch for."

"I sure do. This bump's not bleeding, so I'm going to leave it alone." Smail turned to put away his supplies and tidy the counter.

Caddie sighed and nestled into the pillow. She wouldn't think about Tilley. The captain had trusted her enough to send her out with a detail of six men. She would forget about the boatswain's perpetual scowl and his antipathy to female petty officers.

Maybe after a while, when she wasn't so benumbed, she'd roll over on her side. She couldn't lie on her left side because of her broken arm and the lump on her temple. She'd have to try her right side. Later.

What would her mother say? Her eyelids flew open and she winced. Mom would have fits. Caddie's first long deployment in Alaskan waters, and she'd been injured. Smail seemed to think she'd get several weeks of medical leave. She'd like to go home for a visit, though Mom would fuss over her. Would that be so bad? And would the Coast Guard pay for her flight? Probably not. Of course, if she left Kodiak, she wouldn't see Aven Holland again.

That was a depressing thought. She'd only met the *Milroy*'s boatswain's mate once—at church a few weeks ago—but she'd hoped to see him again soon. Whenever they were both in port again. Which could be tricky when they served on different ships.

But that's good, she sleepily reminded herself. If they were on the same ship, they wouldn't be allowed to date. But since she was on the *Wintergreen* and Aven was on the *Milroy*, they might actually have a chance. . . .

She drifted off into blessed velvety darkness.

❧

Strong hands grabbed Aven and held him up.

"You all right, sir?" Kusiak's strained voice was close to his ear.

Aven pressed the throbbing spot on his abdomen where the punch had landed. He gasped for breath. "Don't call me—"

Reality rushed back to him. Half a dozen fishermen advanced toward them, clenching their fists. One held a knife, and the one with the gaff seemed focused on Aven. He grabbed his radio and pushed the call button. "This is *Milroy* 1. Request immediate aid. We're arresting the crew and impounding this vessel. They're armed and hostile."

"Affirmative," his superior replied. "*Milroy* is en route to *Molly K*, ETA ten minutes."

The briefest glance showed Aven that the cutter was already headed their way and had a Zodiac in the davits so more men could join him on the fishing boat as quickly as possible. The other inspection crews had probably returned to the cutter.

Give me ten minutes, Lord. Let us keep a lid on things for ten minutes.

He held up a hand and spoke firmly. "Stand back. You're under arrest. You'll be taken to shore and turned over to the state police."

The big man swung again, but Aven dodged the blow this time and came up with his pistol in his hand. As he straightened, he heard the smack of bone on flesh beside him, and his four men flew into the fray. Aven alone stood his ground, with his pistol leveled at the big fisherman in the red hat.

Kusiak tumbled into Aven, a gash on the side of his head streaming blood. Aven tilted the pistol and fired a shot just over the big man's head.

"Get back! All of you!"

In the shocked silence, the crew of the *Molly K* hesitated and looked toward their captain. Andrews stood a little apart, near the hatch, and Aven didn't think he'd taken part in the melee. He looked at Aven for a moment then his shoulders wilted.

"Do as he says." The knowledge that he'd lost his boat showed in the tight lines of his face.

The fishermen shuffled toward the bow. Aven's men scrambled to stand beside him again, keeping watchful eyes on their adversaries. Captain Andrews dragged his feet across the deck and turned slowly, standing amid his crew.

"All right, all of you hit the deck, and I mean *now*." Aven swept the pistol in a slow arc in front of him, panning the cluster of glowering men.

His seamen stood around him panting, still coiled tight with unexpended energy. Kusiak swayed. The wound on his temple bled freely, and Aven wondered how the young seaman could stay upright on the rocking boat.

He turned his attention back to the boat's crew. They were waiting, watching the huge man who'd led the confrontation.

"Hit the deck, or I'll drop you," Aven growled. If he lost control now, it was all over. Would he be able to pull the trigger if the man charged him? Yes.

The fishermen stared at him, waiting. The fierce wind buffeted them, pulling at their beards and clothing.

Captain Andrews dropped to his knees. One by one, the other men followed. The big man was the last to go down.

Aven exhaled.

　　　　　　　　　◆

Caddie awoke and looked warily around. The room was too big for a ship's cabin. Slowly the events of the last two days came back to her. The docking in Kodiak and her transfer to the hospital ashore. Surgery.

She grimaced. Her compound fracture required an operation, so the doctor could insert a pin at the elbow. The surgeon had assured her she would heal and be able to resume her duties in six weeks. She'd asked what that would mean as far as her career went, but he hadn't been able to tell her.

She struggled to sit up, but pain lanced through her bandaged arm. Hadn't the doctor said something about putting it in a cast? Not for a few days, she recalled. It would have to wait until the swelling had subsided.

She spotted a button on the bed's side rail and pushed it. The head end of the bed slowly elevated. Progress.

Just as she'd reached a more comfortable level, a nurse entered the room. "Well, good morning! Feeling better?"

"Not really. My arm hurts."

"I'll get your meds." The nurse seemed to have a perpetual smile. Her uniform smock with green and purple dinosaurs might go over better in the children's ward. "Feel like eating breakfast?"

"Uh. . .maybe. What time is it?"

The nurse cocked her head to one side, still smiling. "Just after nine o'clock. It's a little late for breakfast, but I asked them to hold a tray for you."

"Thank you," Caddie said. She put her hand up to her

head. The bump was still there, still sore. "Is it Wednesday?"

"Thursday. They brought you in yesterday and you had your surgery. You've slept a good ten hours."

"Oh." At least they hadn't wakened her every hour, as Smail had done on the ship.

"I'll come right back with your painkillers and breakfast."

The nurse left the room, and Caddie lay back, remembering the arduous rescue of the Russian fishermen.

"I didn't get to see Attu," she said aloud. She had looked forward to seeing the memorial commemorating the only battle fought on American soil in World War II. Her father had described it to her. . .and his mixed feelings of dismay and patriotism when he'd viewed it. Another chance to see the landmark wouldn't come soon.

A soft knock at the door again drew her attention. Aven Holland came in hesitantly, eyeing her with uncertain dark eyes. He held a rolled-up magazine in one hand. "Hi. Remember me?"

She couldn't hold back a grin then realized she was wearing a johnny, in contrast to his neat shipboard work uniform. She grabbed the edge of the coverlet and yanked it up to her collarbone. "Of course. Come on in."

He came closer and stood awkwardly a couple of feet from her bed. "I brought one of the seamen from the *Milroy* in for stitches, and they told me downstairs you were here."

"What happened on the *Milroy*? An accident?"

"Not exactly. We had a little fracas with the crew of a fishing boat. Had to impound the boat and haul them in. Kusiak got cut up a little."

"Wow. Sounds like a bad week for our side." She gazed up at him and her heart fluttered. His concern was evident, as was his discomfort. Could this well-muscled boatswain's mate harbor a shy side? She'd noticed a hesitance about him when they'd first met a few weeks ago, after the adult Sunday school class.

She'd gone to church in town with her friend Jo-Lynn Phifer and her husband. The young couple, who lived a few doors down from Caddie in base housing, had been married a year. Mark Phifer held a slightly lower rank than Caddie, and he served with Aven on the law enforcement cutter *Milroy*.

Aven looked even better than she remembered. And he'd cared enough to come up and see her when he'd heard she was hurt.

"Who did you say told you I was here?"

"I ran into a medic from your ship. Smail."

Caddie nodded. The hospital corpsman must have come to check on her.

"He said you had a tough time on a rescue mission and got smashed up just as you were about to reboard the *Wintergreen*."

"That's about right. A Russian trawler was taking on water. I'm not sure what happened—if they hit something or what. The sea was rough. Anyway, it was about to sink when we got there, and the crew had abandoned ship."

Aven nodded, gazing attentively into her eyes.

Caddie recalled their timid first meeting at church. Small talk, blushing, eyeing each other with speculation—too much like high school. But after they'd parted, she couldn't stop thinking about Aven. Her ship was deployed the next day for more than a month, and she'd received a rapid initiation to life in the Gulf of Alaska, then on into the Bering Sea. She knew Aven and Mark had been out on shorter cruises during that time, inspecting fishing vessels. She'd only been able to hope and pray that they'd be in Kodiak at the same time again when her ship returned to port.

"I wonder where my camera is," she said.

Aven's eyes widened. "Your camera?"

"I had it in my locker on the ship with my clothes and things."

"It's probably still there. I expect one of the *Wintergreen*'s officers will come in today and bring you up to speed. If they have to deploy without you, they'll send your things ashore."

Caddie nodded, trying to follow. Her head throbbed. "So...how long are you here for?" she asked.

"I'm not sure. I've got to fly to the mainland tomorrow. The fishermen we arrested will be arraigned in Anchorage. The police want me on hand in case they need my testimony."

"Doesn't that usually happen at the trial?"

"Well yes, but this is a messy situation. We arrested seven men, and we need to make sure the charges stick for all of them. The police don't want to take a chance of any of them walking, so they want me to give a deposition to the district attorney."

"The fishermen resisted arrest?" Caddie asked.

"Big time. Not the captain. But we'd already charged him with exceeding his limits and safety violations, so he's in custody, too. I'm afraid he's lost his boat for good." He tapped the magazine against his thigh and suddenly seemed to realize he held it. "Oh hey, I picked this up at the gift shop downstairs. Don't know if you like crosswords. . ." He held it out tentatively.

Caddie smiled and reached for it with her good arm. Amazing how much better she felt after just a few minutes of conversation. "Thanks a lot. I don't know how long I'm stuck here for. This might save me from dying of boredom."

"Could have been worse," he said. "I mean, you're not left-handed, are you?"

She chuckled. "No, I'm not."

"Well, listen, I'll be back for the weekend. Unless my ship's called out for an emergency, that is. If you're out of the hospital. . ." He anxiously scanned her face.

"Oh, I think I will be. I hope I can leave today. The

doctor should be in soon to tell me."

"Your arm must hurt."

"It does. They tell me it will for a while."

"I'm sorry about that. Do you think you'll be in church Sunday? Or does your ship go out again?"

She gritted her teeth. "I don't think they'll let me go back on active duty for a while, so I should be there."

"Oh, of course," he said quickly. "I didn't think about that."

"I might get to go home and see my family for a while."

"You should if you can." She looked up at him, and he shrugged. "It's hard sometimes to keep touch with your family."

"Yeah." She wondered how Mom and Jordan and Mira were getting along back in Washington. "I guess it depends on what the doctor and my CO say."

The nurse bustled into the room carrying a tray. "Here we go. Sorry I got held up with another patient for a few minutes." She nodded at Aven. "Hello."

"I guess I'd better get going," he said.

Caddie wished he could stay, but that was silly. He had work to do. "Thanks for coming. It. . .means a lot to me." Had she said too much? She barely knew him.

Aven sucked in a deep breath and glanced toward the nurse. "Well, I hope to see you Sunday."

"Yeah."

He nodded and walked out, his back and shoulders straight.

The nurse gazed after him and sighed. "Now that's a keeper."

Caddie felt a blush rising from the neck of her johnny to the throbbing bump on her head. "Oh, he's just a friend. An acquaintance, I should say."

The nurse handed her a small cup with her pain pills inside. "He's not your CO, is he?"

"No. No, he's on a different ship even." Why did she feel she needed to say that?

The nurse smiled. "Yup. A real keeper."

three

—

Late Friday afternoon, Aven drove a rented SUV into his family's dooryard in Wasilla. The big log house sat squarely against a backdrop of mountains in the distance. He sat for a moment, soaking up the view—his favorite after the open sea.

A dog began to bark, and soon two dozen more picked up the chorus. His sister Robyn came around the corner of the house as the front door opened and Mom came out onto the stoop.

"Aven!" His mother hurried down the steps.

Robyn broke into a run and reached him first, flinging her arms around him.

"Hey, Sis." Aven let her kiss him and then embraced his mother.

"I can't believe you're here. Are you on leave?" Mom pulled away and looked him up and down.

"I had an errand in Anchorage. I have to go back tomorrow and fly out to Kodiak, but I can stay the night."

"Great!" Robyn looped her arm through his. "Come see the pups."

"Whoa. Let him bring his things inside," Mom said with a laugh. "Those dogs aren't going anywhere."

Aven opened the back door of the vehicle and hauled out his bag. He slung it over his shoulder and walked between them toward the log home.

Robyn looked great, as usual, in casual clothes, with her dark hair pulled into a braid. She never wore makeup, but then she'd never needed it. At twenty-two, she'd left the tomboy persona behind, keeping the sturdiness that came

29

from everyday hard work mingled with grace inherited from their mother.

"How's Grandpa doing?" he asked.

His mother wagged her head back and forth, frowning. "He has a lot of pain from his arthritis. Hard to get around. But he wants to help all he can, so we find jobs he can do without too much discomfort."

As Aven entered the house, he struggled once more with the conflict he always experienced when he came home. Should he be here in Wasilla, helping them? Or should he go on with his career? His mother and sister shouldn't have to work so hard.

Grandpa Steve looked up from his recliner in the living room and grinned. "Well, well, well! Look who's here." He leaned forward and pushed on the arms of the chair, then sank back into the cushion with a little moan.

"Don't get up, Grandpa." Aven bent to hug him. "How are you?" He lowered his bag to the floor and sat down on the sagging sofa nearby.

"Awful. Just awful."

"Oh, come on, Dad. Don't be so negative." Aven's mother smiled, but the worry lines on her forehead deepened.

"Do you want me to lie and say I'm doing great? It takes me half an hour to get dressed in the morning."

"At least you can still dress yourself," Robyn said.

"Ha. There is that." Grandpa waved a hand, dismissing their opinions. "If anyone had ever told me how hard it was to get old, I'd have laughed. But now I'm starting to appreciate the old folks."

"You're not old, Grandpa," Aven said.

"Says you." He pulled off his glasses and polished them on his shirttail. "This climate isn't kind to the old bones. I don't know how the pioneers did it."

"You want to move to California?" Mom asked. "Just say

the word, Dad. We'll pack up and move."

"No, don't start that." Grandpa winked at Aven. "Robyn would never go. She won't leave her dogs. And there's not much call for sled dogs in Southern California."

"I'm going to start supper," Mom said. "Aven, put your things in your room."

"I'll be back in a few minutes. I need to finish feeding the dogs," Robyn said, heading for the door.

"I'll help you." Aven rose and reached for his sea bag.

"Better change out of that uniform if you're going out to the kennels with me." Robyn paused with her hand on the doorknob. "I'll meet you by the barn. I was measuring out food when you drove in."

Ten minutes later, Aven met his sister outside wearing frayed jeans that he left at home for times when he had leave. The barn was really only a log shed sturdy enough to secure the dogs' food against marauding bears. Robyn was about to make a trip among the kennels, where the adult dogs were chained to their individual doghouses.

"How many mutts do you have right now?"

"Counting my sled team and alternates, the pups, and the boarders, forty-two."

Aven whistled. "That's a lot of dog food and meat."

"I'll say." Robyn handed him a bucket full of food and pointed to the left side of the kennel yard. "Give those six a scoop each. Boffo and Scooter will be glad to see you."

The dogs were yapping again, demanding their supper. The sun was still high—it would barely sink below the horizon tonight. The dogs didn't seem to mind. After their meal, they would settle down for a snooze.

Aven laughed when Scooter yipped and jumped to the end of his chain. He reached to pat the aging husky's head. "Hey, fella. Long time no see." He stooped down, and Scooter licked his face. The old dog had been Aven's leader when he used to mush during his teen years. Dreams of the Iditarod Trail had faded once Aven joined the Coast Guard, but it was possible his sister still thought about it. The race of more than a thousand miles was every musher's dream. The short race the family had established a decade ago had fed his own interest when he was a teenager. With Robyn, the dog business had become almost an obsession.

He gave Scooter his food and moved on to the next dog.

When all the adults were fed, Robyn grabbed his sleeve and dragged him over to the puppy pens. "Look! Aren't they great?"

"They look terrific. Sold any of this batch yet?"

"Two are reserved. And, Aven, did I tell you? Craig Liston bought one of our two-year-olds last week. JoJo will run in the Iditarod next February."

"Wow, I'm impressed." Aven reached out and tugged Robyn's dark, thick braid. "Selling dogs to champion mushers. How cool is that?"

She grinned, and he thought how pretty his sister was when she wasn't carrying a load of worry. "It's super cool. And Craig and his wife stayed to lunch and talked to us for about an hour about racing."

"That's great. Are you going to enter any races this year?"

Robyn grimaced. "Can't afford to."

"The entrance fees are pretty stiff," Aven agreed.

"Not just that. I need to concentrate on training. I really need some new harness for the clients' dogs, though." Robyn sighed. "I should have one, anyway. People come here when we host the Fire and Ice, and the sponsors are getting around with beat-up old equipment and harness held together with baling twine and bubble gum. That doesn't make people want to buy pups from us or hire us to train their dogs."

"It can't be that bad."

"Nearly." Robyn's eyes flickered. "The profit from last

winter's race only lasted a couple of months. We barely had enough for the last load of dog food. And Dr. Baker let us pay the vet bill in installments."

Again Aven felt a stab of guilt. He'd joined the service over eight years ago expecting to stay in only four years. But he'd discovered that he loved the sea and the life of the Coast Guard. Now that he'd worked his way up to boatswain's mate, he was able to help the family out. Since his father's death, he'd sent almost half his pay home to his mother every month.

But on days like today, when he saw how they struggled, he wondered if he couldn't do more good for the family here at home.

Robyn turned toward the house. "Come on. I shouldn't be whining to you, of all people. You're a huge help to us."

"I'm glad I'm able."

She nodded soberly. "I don't think we'd have made it through last winter without you. Mom wanted to sell all the dogs."

"But then how would you support yourselves?"

Robyn shrugged. "I don't know. Move into Anchorage and find jobs, I guess. But we didn't have to. That's the good news. We got two teams of dogs in to train, and we sold a couple of yearlings. Between that, the Permanent Fund, the money you sent us, and what Mom invested from Dad's insurance, we got by."

"You should have told me things were tight. Maybe I could have done more."

"Well, we're doing okay now. You shouldn't have to put every penny you earn into this place."

Aven followed her back to the shed, where she stowed the buckets and locked the door.

"I'll come back out after supper and refill their water dishes." Robyn took his arm again, as though she wanted to reassure herself that he was actually within reach.

Aven looked back at the now quiet kennels. The dogs had been a hobby when he lived at home. His father had worked for an oil company, and the dog business didn't have to support them while Dad was alive. But now the Holland family lived close to poverty.

"I really need to get home more often," he said. "Grandpa's lost weight."

Robyn nodded. "He had it rough this spring, but I think he's a little better now."

"He won't be able to cut wood this year."

"Well, we still have about three cord left that's nice and dry, but we figured we'd have to buy the rest for next winter—you're right about that."

Aven knew he couldn't get enough time off now to do the job, but maybe he could contribute more to the cost of the fuel. His own expenses were minimal. He was glad he had a pay envelope in his pocket to give his mother. "So, how much does a team harness cost?"

Robyn shrugged. "More than I've got saved so far. I'd like to have a good one when I get it. You know, one that will last and look good to the customers who come to look us over. But don't worry. I'll keep saving my pennies, and someday I'll have it."

ə•

On Sunday morning, Caddie dressed in civilian clothes. She was proud of her uniform, but she also enjoyed wearing her civvies while off duty. Going to church in a dress brought a renewed sense of femininity, something easily lost on a ship with fifty men and only a handful of other women. And when she met people at church, she didn't want the uniform to cloud their perceptions of her. A Coast Guard petty officer's uniform carried expectations.

Of course, the cast on her arm detracted somewhat from

the look she'd hoped for. She studied her reflection in the mirror. Her face wasn't as pale as it had been two days ago, when she'd come home to the tiny one-bedroom apartment she rented in the base housing units. And the snowy white sling would go with any color in her wardrobe.

The memory of a certain boatswain's mate's impromptu visit to the hospital also influenced her choice of outfit and careful grooming that morning. Aven had said he hoped to be back from Anchorage in time for church this weekend. She hadn't expected to meet a charming and eligible man during her assignment in the North. Was meeting Aven one of God's blessings for her?

She closed the closet on the neat row of uniforms, glad that her captain had sent her clothing and camera bag to her apartment the day she left the hospital. Maybe soon she'd feel like taking pictures again.

She walked to the nightstand and picked up the small, pewter-framed photo of herself and her father. Both wore their dress uniforms. Her mother had taken the picture after Caddie's graduation from basic training, and it ranked high among her treasures. "I love you, Dad," she whispered. She brushed back a tear and squared her shoulders.

Mark and Jo-Lynn picked her up right on time, and she dove into the backseat of their decade-old sedan. She was getting used to the awkward cast and moving about without jarring her injured arm.

During the ten-minute drive, she and Mark compared notes on their recent experiences at sea. Though Caddie knew Mark served with Aven, she didn't mention his name.

Neither did Mark. He launched into a tale of woe about his assignment to inspect a crab fishing boat in rough weather. "One man was seasick all day, from the time we boarded that boat. And I thought I'd have frostbite by the time we got done weighing all the crabs."

"Didn't you wear gloves?" Caddie asked.

"Well, yeah, but the cold still gets to you. They did their processing on the deck, and the wind chill was intense."

"Oh, like Caddie doesn't know that. It gets cold at sea up here, even in summer." Jo-Lynn swiveled in her seat and looked at her. "You're lucky you came home at all, girl. You got a crack on the head and a broken arm. You could have drowned."

Caddie nodded. "God protected me."

"Well, I'm glad you weren't hurt worse. Have you told your mother?" Jo-Lynn asked.

"I called her yesterday. She wants me to come home for a while, but I haven't decided yet."

Mark pulled into the parking lot, and they all entered the church together.

"Hey, there's Aven Holland," Jo-Lynn whispered as they walked down the aisle looking for a place to sit. "He's staring at you."

Caddie glanced over the pews to her left and spotted him. She smiled and raised her Bible a little as a substitute wave. She felt her face flush and wished she could have left the sling and cast back in her apartment.

Aven's face lit up, and he returned her wave.

She turned her attention back to Jo-Lynn, knowing her face was scarlet by now. "Do you want to sit here?" She didn't wait for her friend to answer, but scooted into a pew and sat down halfway along the row.

A moment later, Jo-Lynn bent toward her and said, "I think he likes you."

Caddie opened her mouth to respond, but thought better of it and swallowed. She fought the urge to glance across the aisle and back. The music director walked to the podium, and Caddie resolved to keep her attention on the service.

Afterward was a different story, however. As the people

surged into the aisles, Mark made a beeline toward Aven.

In less than a minute, Caddie found herself standing a yard from him as Jo-Lynn and Mark asked him how his trip to Anchorage had gone and if he'd be joining the crew of the *Milroy* when the cutter headed out again Tuesday.

His dark eyes flickered Caddie's way now and then as they talked, and his smile drew her in, too.

"When the pastor was talking about how the Lord abhors dishonest scales, I was thinking of the boat my crew boarded last Wednesday," he said.

Mark chuckled. "Yeah, you got a fellow who abhorred the honest ones, didn't you?"

"That's about the size of it."

"I hear they gave you a lot of trouble," Jo-Lynn said.

"Nothing we couldn't handle."

Caddie shivered. Whose adventure had been worse—hers or Aven's? She was thankful God had brought them both safely to their home port.

Aven wore his uniform today—most of the men did. Probably it was easier for them, especially those who were single, than maintaining a Sunday civilian wardrobe. He was an inch or two taller than Mark, and his short, dark hair lay shiny and clean, parted casually on the left. His shoulders remained straight, even as he relaxed and talked to his friend.

Their conversation turned back to the sermon they'd just listened to. Caddie was mildly surprised but pleased that Aven commented on how the pastor's message about honesty encouraged him to do his job the best that he could, even when it was hard. He seemed like just the kind of man Caddie could go for, but she didn't want to make any assumptions. Personal relationships in the military could be tricky.

Over the past six years, she'd found it best to go by the book. Life was less complicated that way. Besides, at twenty-four years of age, she wasn't sure she wanted to add romantic complications to the frustrations of her career. It was hard enough trying to do everything right when she was on duty—especially when the boatswain watched her every move—and studying the manual and the charts of the waters her ship would sail. Did she have time to think about romance?

Aven looked her way again, and his smile melted the iceberg of doubt in her stomach. If she didn't have time, she would make time.

"Sounds to me like you guys take way too much flak from those fishermen," Jo-Lynn said.

"Oh, I don't know," Aven replied. "They feel intimidated when we board their boats."

"Yeah," Mark said. "Especially when they know they've broken the law. We have to expect a little belligerence."

Aven turned to Caddie. "How's the arm?"

"It still aches some, but the doctor says it will heal well. I'm off duty for at least a month, though. Physical therapy every day."

"So, you said you might go home?" Jo-Lynn asked.

Caddie hesitated, hoping the annoying blush would stay at bay. She didn't want to admit she'd postponed making plans until she knew whether or not she'd have a chance to see Aven again. "I might. Later this week, maybe. Right now I'm taking it easy and getting used to pulling clothes on over a cast."

Aven smiled. "I hope this hasn't soured you on Alaska."

"Oh, no. I'm glad I was assigned here. Sometimes I feel a bit. . ." She struggled for the right word and shrugged. "Inadequate for the job, I guess. But. . .the Lord is always there."

He nodded solemnly. "That's right. He's there for us even when we're weak."

Caddie straightened her shoulders a little. She would keep doing her best and focus on God's promises when she needed help in pleasing her exacting superiors. She had chosen this life, and she needed to do it well.

An image of her father flashed through her mind. He had sailed these same waters and met the same challenges she faced now. Her service was a memorial to her dad. Had she inadvertently added another layer of expectation to her workload? Did wanting to honor Dad increase the stress of her job?

"There are times when I think I make the job harder than it really is." As soon as the words came out, she regretted voicing the thought.

But Aven's eyes glinted as he nodded. "That's easy to do. Especially when we forget who's really in charge. Remember to rely on His strength."

"Well, hey, why don't we go get something to eat?" Jo-Lynn asked.

"Yeah," Mark said, "if we can find a place that's not too full of tourists."

"I know a seafood place," Aven said. "We might have to wait a little while for a table, but the food is good and it's not too expensive."

"Let's go." Jo-Lynn herded them all into the parking lot and nudged Caddie toward Aven's truck. "Go ahead with Aven. We'll follow you."

Caddie felt her face warm again, but Aven smiled. "Sure, if you don't mind my pickup. It's practically old enough to vote." He opened the passenger door for her and offered his hand. "Can you manage with that cast? I don't want you to hurt your arm."

"Thanks." As she reached for his hand, her stomach fluttered. His strong, warm fingers clasped hers, and he gave her just enough leverage to make her climb into the cab quick and painless. She wondered if he felt as nervous as she did. If so, he didn't show it.

four

The harborside restaurant was crowded when they arrived shortly before one o'clock, but Aven didn't mind. He used the wait for a table as a chance to learn more about Caddie. She looked terrific in a muted green dress, and her hair seemed shiny and a little poufier than usual. He wondered if it felt soft.

"You like seafood?" he asked.

"Yeah. Do you?"

He nodded. "I've seen a lot of salmon lately, though. I'm not sure I want to eat it today." He eyed her, wondering what to ask next. There were so many things he wanted to know about her.

Mark and Jo-Lynn were conveniently studying a menu on the wall.

"See, they have beef and chicken, too," Jo-Lynn said.

Aven looked at Caddie and took a deep breath. "So you're heading home to recuperate?"

"If the doctor says I can and if I can line up physical therapy there."

"Where's home?"

"Washington." She added quickly, "The state, not D.C."

"Beautiful place to live. Your folks live there?"

"Just my mom, my brother, and sister."

Did that mean her parents were divorced? Not the best time to ask. Aven nodded and passed his key ring from his right hand to his left. He realized he'd done that about twenty times in the two minutes they'd stood waiting. He wasn't sure he'd even be able to eat. He shoved the key ring into his pocket. "If you're going to be in town tomorrow. . ."

"I'm taking her to the Baranov Museum tomorrow," Jo-Lynn said.

"Oh."

Mark poked Jo-Lynn with his elbow.

"What?" she asked.

"Aven has tomorrow off."

"So?" Jo-Lynn looked at Aven and back at Mark. "Oh. Sorry."

Caddie said nothing, but her gaze never left Aven's face. Suddenly he wished he was elsewhere. Jo-Lynn could be a nuisance. Of course, he probably wouldn't have had the nerve to ask Caddie to lunch if Jo-Lynn hadn't instigated the outing.

"That's okay," he said to Jo-Lynn, flashing a glance Caddie's way. "I wasn't going to do anything special tomorrow. I just plan to run a couple of errands."

"Caddie and I could do the museum another time." Jo-Lynn raised her eyebrows at Caddie with an "up-to-you" expression.

Aven gulped and dared to look steadily at Caddie. "I was going to go look over a dog harness for my sister. She needs a new one and she really can't afford it, but she heard about someone not far from here who will put together a custom harness at a reasonable price. She called him for an estimate a few weeks ago and decided it was too spendy, but I said I'd check into it." He looked away. "I thought you might be interested in going along, but. . ."

"Hey, *you* could take Caddie to the museum," Mark said.

"Oh, no," Aven said quickly. "Then Jo-Lynn wouldn't get to go."

Jo-Lynn waved away his objections. "I've seen it three or four times, while you guys were out to sea. I just thought if the weather's nice, Caddie and I could ride into town and take a look. The Baranov has tons of exhibits from the times when the Russians were here, but I don't need to see it again."

"Well. . ." Aven swallowed and turned his attention back to Caddie. "What do you think? We could swing by the harness maker's shop and then see the museum. If you want to. I mean, it might be fun." He stopped talking. Why was it so easy to give orders to a dozen seamen—male or female—on the ship without tripping over his tongue, but a simple invitation to a woman came out all mangled? In his years in uniform, he'd had only a handful of bona fide dates. Was it any wonder, when he couldn't offer a pretty woman a simple sentence without bumbling?

The hostess approached them with a brilliant smile. "Phifer party?"

Mark sprang to attention. "Right here."

As they fell in to follow her to their table, Caddie tossed a smile Aven's way, eyeing him from beneath her lowered lashes. "I'd like that. Thanks."

He barely heard her, but it was enough to send his ego soaring through the roof of the restaurant.

When they reached the table, he pulled out a chair for Caddie. She again smiled at him as she slid into the seat, holding her left arm cautiously away from the edge of the table.

Aven's stomach settled down. Talking to women on land wasn't so hard. Why had he anticipated an afternoon of indigestion? He might even order a steak.

❧

When they entered the harness shop the next day, Caddie stopped just inside the door and inhaled deeply. The leather and oil smells reminded her of a saddle shop she'd visited once. A man who appeared to be in his thirties, with his blond hair pulled back in a ponytail and about two weeks' growth of beard, worked at a raised counter. Aven approached him, and Caddie drifted to a side wall where tooled purses, soft briefcases, dog collars, and leather cuff bracelets hung on display racks.

"My sister, Robyn Holland, called you a couple of weeks ago about a harness," Aven said.

The owner laid down his tools and nodded. "Yeah, I remember." He stuck out his hand. "Brett Sellers."

Aven shook his hand and introduced himself.

"Let me see. . ." Brett thumbed through a card file on the desk. "I quoted her a price on a complete set for ten dogs."

"That's right. She gave you the sizes?"

Caddie surreptitiously studied Aven's profile. He was about four inches taller than she was—five-eleven, she guessed—and even now, trying to act casual about his sister's errand, he maintained the officer's posture. His dark hair reflected the overhead lighting. The contrast between his precise grooming and Sellers's scruffy aura made her smile. Aven's clean-shaven cheeks were smooth, and his firm jaw had just enough roundness to give the impression he was not too pliable, not too obstinate. He wore his jeans and Henley pullover as well as he did his uniform.

"Yes, I think I have all the information I'll need," the harness maker told Aven as he came from behind his counter. "Doesn't your family host one of the smaller races every year?"

"Yeah, the Fire and Ice. My folks have organized that race for the last ten years."

"Never been to it, but I've heard of it."

"It's a fun race. Only a hundred miles, but it's got interesting terrain. Some of the mushers like to use it as a warm-up."

"It's earlier than the Iditarod?"

"Yeah. Middle of January."

Brett lifted a bundle of nylon straps and hardware and

placed it on the counter. "This is the style I recommended to her. She said she wanted good quality, but nothing fancy."

Aven smiled. "That's Robyn. She doesn't want to spend any more than she has to, but she wants good stuff. She's been getting by with old, patched equipment."

"Can't do that on the trail," Brett said.

Caddie stepped forward, eyeing the heap of harness in surprise. "I thought it would all be leather."

Brett grinned. "Things have changed a lot over the years. Dog harnesses are lighter and more durable now. Leather deteriorates faster than synthetics, it stretches more, and it takes longer to dry out. Besides, dogs like to chew it. I love doing leatherwork, but I put together dog harnesses as a sideline. I've done a few custom leather harnesses for show dogs, but for real work, you want nylon or cotton webbing and lots of padding around the collar."

They chatted for a few more minutes, and Caddie listened as Aven told the artisan a little more about his family and the annual race they sponsored.

"I used to get around to some of the races when I lived in Fairbanks," Brett said. He pointed out a few of the nicer points of the sturdy harness.

Aven fingered the straps and nodded. "Okay, I'll take it. Can you put together what she needs while I wait, or should I come back?"

Brett grinned. "I had a feeling when she called Saturday and said her big brother would come look it over, so I took a look at the inventory. I just need a couple more components. I can have the full set ready in a couple of days."

Aven laughed. "She called again? She didn't tell me."

"Yes, she did. I'll have everything ready to her specifications." Brett rang up the purchase, and Aven paid for it.

"Why did you move out here?" Aven asked. "Not many mushers live on the islands."

"My girlfriend's family lives out here. She didn't like Fairbanks, so I agreed to move down here with her. I kind of like it here." Brett nodded toward the display wall. "I don't sell as many harnesses as I used to when I lived up there. I sell more tooled bags and dog leashes now than I do harness. But I do a fair amount of business over the Internet, and sometimes people call me for special orders."

Aven and Caddie went out to the aging pickup. Aven opened the door for her and helped her up carefully. She held on to her cast as she scooted into the cab.

"How's the arm doing?"

"Not too bad." She checked her watch. Not time for her medication yet.

Aven headed the truck toward the center of Kodiak.

"That was nice of you to get the harness for Robyn," Caddie said.

He flexed his shoulders. "Well, she needs it. The sponsors shouldn't show up on race day with equipment tied together with twine. She's saved up about two-thirds of the price, and I can kick in the rest."

"It sounded as though she may have guessed you'd do that."

"I didn't think so, but maybe I'm more predictable than I thought." Aven shook his head, smiling. "She was disappointed because she thought she had enough money, but prices were higher than she expected. She told me when I was home last weekend that she'd shopped online, but she couldn't find a set as good as she wanted for anywhere near what she could afford. So I said I'd come look at what this guy had to offer and see if it was well made and worth waiting for."

Caddie smiled. "She'll be so happy when she gets it."

"Yeah. I think I'll ship it to her. I'd like to take it to her myself, but I doubt I'll get home again before the end of summer. It's rare to get two or three days off together this time of year."

Caddie nodded. No need for explanations when they both understood exactly what life was like for Coast Guard personnel during tourist and fishing seasons. Either of their ships could be called at a moment's notice for search and rescue details. The one constant in their lives was unpredictability.

"The mountains here are unbelievable," she said, peering out the window.

"Yes, this is easily one of the most beautiful places on earth." Aven grinned at her. "Too bad the weather's so nasty most of the year."

"I expect I'll get my fill of it next winter, but it's green and beautiful right now."

"The Coast Guard will probably send you to the Fisheries Law Enforcement School for a few weeks during the worst of the winter."

Caddie glanced down at her cast and scrunched up her face. "Too bad I can't do it now, while my arm is keeping me from active duty. Hey, did I hear you say you're from Wasilla?"

"A few miles outside of town. My folks bought the place when I was little, back when Dad worked for the oil company."

"So you grew up there."

Aven nodded. "Yeah. Robyn was born here in Alaska, at the hospital in Anchorage. I'm a transplant from Pennsylvania, but I don't remember anything about it back there. I think I was two when we moved."

"My family's been all over, but we were in Washington when Dad died, so we stayed there."

"What happened to your dad?"

She pulled in a deep breath, determined not to get teared

up talking about it. "He was in the Coast Guard. Don't know if you knew that."

"No, I didn't."

"Yeah. He actually died while he was on duty." She didn't like to think about it. Remembering how he'd lost his life brought on the doubts she regularly battled. If Dad wasn't tough enough, why should she think she was? "He served in Alaska for two years. At Homer."

"Really?" Aven slowed for a turn. "When?"

"A long time ago. Right before I was born. He was transferred all over the map afterward, but he kept talking about it and saying he'd like to come back. He loved it here."

"I can understand that." Aven eyed her cautiously. "So. . . he didn't die while he served in Alaska?"

"No. He was posted at Seattle when it happened." She smiled, hoping she could keep the tears in submission. "He talked a lot about coming back here. My mom didn't really want to come, though. She didn't like Alaska. She said Washington was far enough north for her."

"Was she depressed? Seasonal affective disorder?"

"Is that the same as light deprivation sickness?"

"Yeah. The fancy name they use for it now."

"Maybe. She didn't like it and said she just wanted to hole up in winter and not go outside when it was dark."

"How do you like it so far?"

"Oh, I like it. Of course, I've only seen the days-in-overdrive part."

He laughed, and she felt encouraged to go on.

"I've always wanted to come here. Probably because of things Dad told us. I decided to get posted in Homer if I could. Kodiak was as close as I could get, but my ship was in Homer a few weeks ago. The *Wintergreen* stopped there to leave off some buoys, and I got to see a little of the town."

"It's beautiful there," Aven said.

"I'll say. The bay is absolutely gorgeous. All those volcanic mountains, and the spit running out into the water. . ." It was easier talking about the incredible terrain than Dad. If Aven would just drop the subject, she'd feel better.

"So, your dad was an officer."

There it was again. "Yeah. He served thirty years. His last command was as skipper of a cutter out of Seattle. He used to joke that he'd served in nearly every district the Coast Guard has."

Aven kept his eyes on the road. "So. . .you've signed on for a career?"

"Probably. It's what I've always wanted to do. Well, since I was ten or so. I wanted to be just like Dad. I knew I couldn't serve under him, but I figured when we had leave together, we could talk about our life at sea. I thought it would be so neat, wearing the uniform just like he did." She smiled at her naiveté. "Dad's death gave me second thoughts."

"How so?" He pulled up at a stop sign and looked over at her.

Caddie shrugged, trying to marshal her thoughts. How much did she want to reveal? Too much might drive Aven away.

Dad had been away a lot during her childhood. It was only lately that she'd thought her ambition might be misplaced. Had the little girl thought somehow that joining the Coast Guard would bring her father closer in a way that would make up for all the times he was away at sea? While she was serving out of Woods Hole, Massachusetts, and her father was posted in Seattle, he'd been killed in the line of duty. Her unplanned visit home for his funeral had broken her heart. She'd returned to duty more determined than ever to make him proud.

She shook her head over the memories and frowned. "Sometimes I want badly to advance and become an officer.

To be a captain, even. But then other days, I know I could never live up to my dad's record, so why even try?"

Aven checked for traffic and pulled forward. "Do you like the Coast Guard?"

"Sailing is fantastic, and the job is challenging. What I'm doing now is the hardest thing I've ever done, but. . .yeah, I like it."

He smiled, and she found herself smiling, too.

"So, what's there to fret about?" he asked.

She lowered her chin and looked toward the green mountainsides and distant gray waves. "I'm always second-guessing myself. Did I really do that right? Can I perform to my CO's expectations? Would Dad be proud of me if he were here?"

"I think I can answer that last one."

She stared at him, weighing whether or not he was serious. "Okay, how?"

"I'm sure he'd be very proud of you now."

"You can't know that."

"I think I can. A father who sees his child trying to emulate him, especially in an area where he excelled and was respected. . .yeah, that's something to be proud of."

"Thanks. I'll remember that next time I wonder if I'm doing this for the wrong reason." She blinked back the rogue tears that filled her eyes. "So, what about your dad? Is he still with the oil company?"

Aven shook his head. "He was flying on business a few years ago. His plane crashed."

Caddie caught her breath. "I'm so sorry." If they could only have one thing in common, that would have been the last thing she'd chosen. Yet his words took on deeper value because of it.

"How's your mom doing?" she asked after a long silence.

"All right. It's been hard. She and Robyn are getting

along, though. I help them when I can."

"Does your mother work?"

"Yes, at home. The dog kennels were a hobby when Dad was alive, but it started turning a profit. Robyn's a very good trainer. She and Mom have kept things going. My grandfather lives there, too. He helps a little, but he can't do much now. Mom got Dad's insurance, and she has a small income from his retirement fund. Like I said, they get by. Just."

"That's a heavy load to carry."

"It can be. Sometimes I think I should leave the Coast Guard and go home to help them. Or get a better paying job somewhere. But so far, I don't feel God's leading me to do those things. So I keep on." He huffed out a breath and smiled. "So. . .do you still want to take in the Baranov Museum? We're almost there."

"I'd like that. I've heard so much about the Russian occupation and heritage, I'd like to learn more."

"You got it." He put on his turn signal and turned in at the museum's parking area.

He was out of the truck and around to her door while Caddie still fumbled with the seat belt release.

He opened the door and leaned on it, grinning at her. "Let's not get too weepy about our families, okay? This is going to be a fun day."

"I won't if you won't." She was glad her tears had cleared up without spilling over. "I am sorry about your dad, though. I'll pray for your mother and Robyn."

"Thanks. I'll pray for your family, too. Now, let's go see what made old Alexander Baranov such a big shot around here."

five

Aven carefully taped up the box with the dog harness for shipping and prepared a label. When he'd finished, he sat down to write a note to Robyn.

Hey Sis,
I went to Brett Sellers's shop and took a look at his work.
I like him, and I think a set of his harness is just what
you need. He put one together, and I picked it up today.
I'll ship it to you tomorrow morning, so watch for a big
box.

He paused and read over what he'd written. He wasn't given to long reports on his activities. He called home now and then and e-mailed when he had a chance. Should he mention that Caddie had gone with him to the harness shop? When he'd gone home last Friday, Caddie was just a breath of hope. Now her presence in his life was a reality.

But if he said anything about her, he'd have to explain who she was and why she rode along and what they'd done for the rest of the day. And a gazillion other things. If he didn't lay it all out there, Robyn would call five minutes after she received the letter, breathless and eager to know all about the "new girlfriend." Which was sort of a joke. No one knew better than Robyn how rarely Aven dated.

Best not to mention Caddie yet, he decided. If things didn't work out, it would be too embarrassing to explain why. Yet, after today. . . His pulse jumped as he remembered how much fun they'd had, lingering in the museum until they'd thoroughly viewed every exhibit. He'd talked her into lunch. She'd insisted she wasn't tired but had taken some painkillers at the restaurant.

Afterward they'd gone to a bookstore where they spent another hour browsing and talking nineteen to the dozen about books they'd read and whatever else came to mind. Inconsequential things somehow had become fascinating when he discussed them with Caddie. She'd admitted at last that she was tired, and he'd reluctantly driven her back to the base.

Aven wished he could see her again, but he had to be on the bridge of the *Milroy* at 0500. And she would fly to Seattle in a couple of days to visit her family for several weeks.

He would miss her. He'd never felt this way about a girl before. Okay, woman. Boatswain's mate third class. His laugh echoed in his empty apartment. Most of the women he'd met since joining the military were either off-limits or nonbelievers. Caddie was not only single and close enough to his rank so they could socialize, but she was a Christian. And she'd promised to drop him a postcard from Washington. He drew in a deep breath, thinking about that. He could look forward to that postcard waiting for him when he came in from his deployment next week.

How long would she be gone from Alaska? She'd said the doctor recommended six weeks off duty, but her captain had suggested she go back to light duty after four, if the surgeon okayed it then. Time would tell.

The letter lay unfinished on the desk. He wouldn't mention Caddie until after she came back to Kodiak. A lot could happen in a month, and he didn't want to get Robyn and his mother all excited about possibilities and have to disappoint them later.

Any time he'd had serious thoughts about a girl before, it hadn't worked out. Caddie was different, and he felt different—more alive and optimistic because of knowing her. Caddie intrigued him more now than she had when he first met her. Even so, he wasn't ready to believe it would last. It was too soon to hope too much. He picked up the pen.

> *It was great seeing you all last weekend. Wish I could come home for a longer visit. Maybe next month. This fall for sure. How's Grandpa doing? Sold any more pups lately?*

He scrawled a couple more lines on his letter and signed it. He would hug the day with Caddie to himself for a while. If things progressed, he'd let Robyn in on it later.

❧

Caddie enjoyed her visit at home and treated her physical therapy sessions as a new challenge. Soon she was out walking daily around the small town outside Seattle, with her camera slung around her neck. She'd picked up photography as a child and loved finding just the right angle for a nature shot. Aspects of light and shade intrigued her. Birds and animals comprised her favorite subjects, and she wished she'd had more time to take photos in Alaska. Every day at home, she walked to the river half a mile away to capture the moods of the water on film. She looked forward to returning to Alaska and photographing its wild waters in all their fury and beauty.

By the end of the second week, when her younger sister, Mira, and brother, Jordan, left for camp, she wandered aimlessly about the house. She did as much housework as her healing arm would allow, while her mother was gone to work during the day, and walked longer distances to stay in shape. She missed her teenage siblings, but she was glad they had the chance for an adventure.

"We should have cancelled the kids' camp reservations,"

her mother said at supper one evening. "You don't have anyone to talk to while I'm at work. If we'd known you would be home—"

"No, I'm fine. I've found people to chat with when I go walking. And anyway, the kids have looked forward to camp for months. You couldn't change that." Caddie resolved to try to keep her impatience better camouflaged.

She'd sent Aven the promised postcard, depicting the Seattle skyline, and written her home address at the bottom. For nearly two weeks, nothing happened, but at last a return postcard came from him. A Kodiak bear nudged her cub up a verdant hillside. Caddie stared at it for a long time. She wished she had taken that picture. Even more, she wished she was back on the island.

That night she at last told her mother about Aven and showed her the postcard.

"Ah, now I see," was her mother's response.

"See what?" Caddie turned the card over and read his innocuous message again:

> We're in port for 2 days, then out again. The usual
> mayhem. Hope the arm's better.
> Aven

No revelations there.

Her mother smiled. "Tell me more about him."

To her own surprise, Caddie talked nonstop for ten minutes about Aven—what he looked like, his manners, his family, his faith, and his love of the sea.

"If you went back early, would you be able to see him?" Mom asked.

"I don't know. His ship could be out for weeks."

"But there's a chance."

"I suppose." Caddie nodded with a rueful smile. "You're

right. If I go back, I'll be close by if his ship docks again."

"You should go."

She eyed her mother's placid features. "It's not like we've dated a lot, Mom. Only that one time."

"But it won't happen again if you stay here."

"Well. . .you wouldn't mind?"

Her mother shook her head. "I'll miss you, of course. I always do when you're gone. But it seems to me it's important to you. You need to do this."

&

When Caddie stood again on the dock at the base in Kodiak the following Monday, she knew she'd taken the right course. Her own ship's vacant berth gaped along one side of the pier. The *Milroy* was also at sea, but she needed no more than five minutes at the PX chatting with the wives of some of the seamen on board to tell her they expected the cutter to return by the weekend.

She spent the afternoon unpacking and setting up more physical therapy sessions and a checkup with her surgeon. She took out her camera and the new telephoto lens she'd bought in Seattle. Maybe this would be a good time to get some wildlife close-ups.

Jo-Lynn drove her to the doctor's office the next morning.

Caddie studied the surgeon's face as carefully as he examined her arm. Would he pronounce her fit for duty? What if her arm had been permanently weakened by the injury?

"Does that hurt?"

"No."

"How about now?"

She winced. "A little."

"When does your ship deploy next?" he asked, flexing her elbow gently while he fingered the joint.

"Not for eight days. It's scheduled to dock Saturday and go out again next Wednesday."

"Hmm."

What was that supposed to mean? She watched his eyes keenly.

The doctor's dark brows contracted as he extended her arm again. "I want to leave the cast on another week. You're not ready to lift or tug on ropes yet."

She smiled. He obviously hadn't much sailing experience. "But after a week? Can I go back to sea then?"

"I can't say for sure." He turned on his stool and consulted his computer screen. "The trouble with active duty is that they expect you to be active. They want you to do everything you did before your medical leave. But we want to avoid reinjuring that arm at all costs. Better to take a longer leave than to go back too soon."

"So. . .when will we know?"

He swiveled to face her again. "Come in Monday. I'll want another X-ray then. I'll send a copy of my report to your CO today, but I'm recommending at least another week of sick leave. We'll see how things look then. You may be able to resume light duty. And don't worry about it. Relax. See some sights. This is the best time of year to see Alaska. Enjoy it."

&

"This is the U.S. Coast Guard. Heave to." Lieutenant Greer, the skipper of the *Milroy*, spoke into the public address system, hailing the crew of a small cabin cruiser that danced over the waves in front of them. Beside him, Aven watched the small, quick boat dash for shallow water.

Greer brought his fist down on the wooden rail. It was plain to all that the vessel's crew defied him. The boat the *Milroy* pursued wasn't going to slow down, let alone heave to and let them board.

"You want us to fire a warning shot?" Aven asked.

Greer, who enjoyed the courtesy title of "captain" on the law enforcement cutter, shook his head. "Too close to shore. We don't want any accidents."

Aven stood beside his skipper on the bridge, watching helplessly as the runaway boat churned for a strait between two islands. "We can't follow them through there, sir. The tide's not high enough."

"Are you sure?" His skipper looked over his shoulder at him.

"Not unless the tide's high."

Greer frowned. "It's close."

The truth was the tide had turned an hour ago and the channel they raced toward would only let the 110-foot cutter escape without scars under ideal conditions. "Too risky." Aven's stomach clenched when he pictured what could happen if they tried it.

The skipper swore. "How long to go around to the east?"

Aven did some rapid calculations. "Too long."

The shores of the hilly, tree-covered islands drew closer. Aven's pulse thudded. If he were Officer of the Deck, he would never risk taking the cutter in so far an hour past high tide. He started to speak again but thought better of it. Couldn't contradict the captain.

As the smaller boat disappeared around a point of land, Greer called, "Change course."

Aven exhaled. They would survive to settle things with the boat's owners another day.

The cutter swung around, but the usually agile ship seemed to catch itself and stall. A loud crunch drew everyone's gaze to Greer. A shudder ran through the hull. The captain swore again. "Holland, get below and find out what's going on."

Aven ran for the ladder. As he scrambled down to the engine room three decks below, he could tell the *Milroy* had freed itself and was not hung up on anything below the waves. That was a relief. But there was bound to be some damage.

The chief engineer met him in the doorway to the engine room and assured him they weren't taking on water. "May have some trouble with the prop, though."

Twenty minutes later, Aven climbed more slowly up the ladders. He'd already reported to the bridge by radio. The boatswain had joined Greer. It was nearly time for the shift to change, and he would replace the captain as Officer of the Deck. The cutter moved sluggishly through the sea, and Aven didn't have to ask to know they were headed for Kodiak and repairs.

"You got that boat's call numbers, right?" Greer called as Aven entered.

"Aye, aye, sir." He'd given the information to the operations specialist before they'd scraped bottom, but he didn't say so. Greer's expression was sour enough. Aven walked over to the ops specialist's computer console.

The man rapidly keyed information into the computer and scanned the results. "Got it, sir. They're out of Larsen Bay."

"Larsen Bay?"

"Affirmative."

The town of about a hundred residents lay on the west side of Kodiak Island and catered to sport fishermen. Bears and salmon canning, that's what the village was best known for. Several commercial fishing boats operated out of there.

"Should we contact the state police?" Aven asked. Something about the Larsen Bay connection teased at his memory. When Greer hesitated, he shrugged. "We don't have proof they were smuggling. It was an anonymous tip."

The skipper turned toward the hatch. "Wouldn't hurt to let them go rattle the owner's cage. I'll be in my quarters."

Aven recorded the afternoon's events in the log, including the short-lived pursuit of the cabin cruiser. Occasionally citizens called in tips about illegal activities on the water, and the Coast Guard was expected to follow up on them. The fact that this boat's crew hadn't wanted to stick around and answer questions lent some credulity to the informant's call.

He hated adding that the *Milroy*'s propeller was damaged in the pursuit. That wouldn't look well for Greer. Overeager. Aven hoped the skipper wouldn't get into trouble over it. And it meant their deployment would be cut short. No telling how long repairs would take. If Caddie had been within a thousand miles, he'd have looked forward to docking in Kodiak, but she was probably still in Washington with her family.

&

Chicken noodle soup and a sandwich. Caddie decided to save money and eat in her apartment Thursday evening. Maybe tomorrow she'd ask around to see how much it would cost to fly to one of the best bear-watching spots on the island. She'd probably never have a better chance. She'd regret it if she left Alaska without at least trying to get some good Kodiak bear pictures.

The doorbell rang.

She turned off the burner, hurried to the door, and looked through the peephole. For a moment she doubted her eyesight. Quickly, she threw the deadbolt. "Aven! You're not supposed to get in until Saturday."

He clenched his teeth as he smiled. "We're back early. The *Milroy* needs repairs."

Caddie arched her eyebrows and held the door wider. "What happened? Nothing serious, I hope."

"Not really, but it will take a few days to fix." He stepped inside. "We got a little close to shore, and the propeller hung up on a rock."

"That's too bad."

"Yeah. So anyway, Mark called me a few minutes ago and said Jo-Lynn told him you were back. I hope you don't mind."

"Not a bit."

Aven took off his hat and looked around. "I'd say, 'Nice place you've got here,' but it looks just like my place."

She laughed. "Thanks. I think the one-bedroom units are all alike."

"That's a nice picture, though." He stepped closer to the framed photograph she'd hung between the two living room windows when she moved in.

"Thanks. That's my brother, Jordan, and his dog. I took it a couple of years ago when I went home on leave. They're both a lot bigger now."

"You took that? It's great."

Caddie looked at it critically. She liked it, too. Jordan at twelve, hugging the half-grown border collie pup. She'd caught both their expressions just right.

Aven swung around, his dark eyes gleaming. "It's terrific. Hey, I wondered if you'd like to go get something to eat."

Caddie thought fleetingly of the soup she'd started to fix. She couldn't ask him to share that and a peanut butter sandwich. The flush that zipped into her cheeks told her she wasn't ready to offer to cook for him in her apartment anyway.

"Well, sure. But. . ." She hesitated. Aven lived frugally to help his family. "If you'll let me pay my share."

He shuddered, his eyes twinkling. "Let's not do that I'll-pay-no-I'll-pay thing."

"Exactly. We'll both pay."

He held out a moment longer, making a comical face.

"Burgers." She tried to put enticement into the one word, and he fell for it.

"Okay, let's go."

She laughed and grabbed her purse and a sweater.

When they reached the restaurant, the tables were jammed with tourists.

"We could eat in the truck." Aven's plaintive tone caught at her heartstrings.

"Okay. That way, we'll be able to hear each other without yelling."

His face cleared and he smiled at her as they waited in line to order their food. The buzz of conversation around them made talking pointless, so she waited silently, but standing beside him sheared away the tedium. Ten minutes later they climbed back into his truck. He pulled out a cup holder rack, and Caddie fumbled with her good hand to situate the drinks.

Aven asked a brief blessing and handed her a wrapped sandwich. "Need help getting that open?"

"I think I can do it." Over the past three weeks, she'd developed an amazing one-handed agility, using the cast as a prop. "Do I dare ask how your ship came to grief?"

He gave a short laugh and shook his head. "It wasn't my fault, for which I'm extremely thankful."

"Oh, yeah. I know the exact feeling."

"We got a tip that a boat carrying drugs would be heading into a certain harbor this morning. It was a long shot that we'd find the right boat, since it was a small one, and you know what it's like looking for a little boat in the Gulf of Alaska, but we found her. Trouble was she was already pretty close to shore when we spotted her and hugging the coast. When we hailed her, she scooted for a channel we couldn't navigate."

"Terrific."

"Yeah." Aven took a bite of his cheeseburger and chewed thoughtfully. A moment later he reached for his cup and looked over at her. "There's something about that boat that bothers me a lot."

"Oh?"

"We traced the registration number. It belongs to a fellow who lives in Larsen Bay. I was assigned to call the state police when we docked, so they can check it out. And guess what?"

"No idea." She waited, knowing he would give her the rest of the story when he was ready.

Aven shifted in his seat and inhaled deeply. "The guy who owns the boat has the same last name as the fisherman who tried to deck me a month ago on the *Molly K.*"

"Same man?"

"His brother."

Caddie gave a soft whistle. "Is the fisherman in jail?"

"No. He should be. Most of them were fined. The big guy—his name's Spruce Waller—did ten whole days in the slammer. The guy who roughed up Seaman Kusiak is still in there—he'll serve 45 days and then a year's probation. The captain lost his boat and got a stiff fine."

"Sounds like he's suffering more than the rest, and you told me he didn't take part in the fight."

"That's right. The laws we have do that sometimes. It's too bad in a way. But this Waller character didn't have a record—which I find incredible, given his temper—and they let him off easy."

Caddie sighed. "And now his brother shows up in your sights."

"Right. It's got me wondering if Spruce, being out of work in the fishing biz, has started something new with his brother. I didn't see him on the boat we were after, but that doesn't mean anything. I didn't know when we were chasing them that his brother owned the boat, so I wasn't looking for him. He's a big guy, though. Six-two or so, and he must weigh around two-fifty."

"His brother may be hefty, too. Maybe they'd look similar from a distance."

"True. And there's another thing. I was thinking that when I went to his indictment, they said Spruce Waller had a cabin in Larsen Bay. But it turns out his place is in *Anton* Larsen Bay, which isn't far from here."

"But his brother lives in Larsen Bay, on the other end of the island?"

"Yeah, pretty much. You can't drive there from here."

"Still, it would be easy to go back and forth in a boat."

"No, too difficult. But it makes it less likely that the brothers are working together. Spruce's main residence is here in Kodiak, and his cabin is fifteen miles away." Aven popped the last bite of his burger into his mouth and crumpled the wrapper. After swallowing, he said, "That was good. Now how about dessert?"

Caddie chuckled. "Not for me, but go ahead. I'll wait here while you get it."

Aven left, and she settled back in the seat, looking out at the ocean view. The sun was still high in the sky. Most of the fishing boats were out, but pleasure craft dotted the harbor. A gull landed on the trash bin a few yards away, and once again she wished she'd brought her camera.

Aven returned a few minutes later, and the bird flew off with a scrap of a bun in its mouth. He held out a steaming cup to her. "Here. I remembered you like hot tea from that time at the restaurant."

"Thank you! That's very thoughtful."

He settled in beside her and put his own coffee in the rack while he opened a pastry package. "Sure you don't want some?"

"No, but thanks."

"You know, this whole thing with the Waller brothers is working on me. I'm trying not to obsess over it."

"Taking it personally?"

"Maybe." Aven frowned. "I shouldn't have let things get out of control on the fishing boat. I wasn't alert enough, and I let him get too close."

"It happens."

"Yeah. I was trying to radio in, and he took advantage of that second's distraction. Kusiak got cut up because of that."

"Is he okay now?"

"Yeah. He'll have an intriguing scar. The rest of us got bruised up a little, but. . ."

"But you're still mad about it?"

"Not mad exactly." He gazed at her then shrugged in defeat. "I've been praying about it. I don't want to go out there having it in for someone. Anger leads to mistakes. But I admit it bothers me that it happened on my watch."

"You could be right about what Waller's doing now, though. His brother may have talked him into running drugs with him. Maybe he can't get another job fishing because of his arrest."

"Naw, I doubt that. There are so many fishing outfits around. And we don't have proof they were carrying drugs. Just an anonymous tip."

"That boat ran from you, and it was definitely the brother's boat, right?" She watched his pensive eyes. He'd already considered that, she could see, and he didn't like the implications.

"Yeah, there was something going on that they didn't want us to know about, that's for sure. If I have anything to say about it, we'll catch up with them one of these days." He looked up and smiled. "Hey, let's forget about them for now. There's still hours of daylight left. It'll hardly even get dark tonight. What do you say we drive over to Fort Abercrombie?"

"I'd love to! I haven't seen it yet."

"Great. The stuff that's left from the World War II era is interesting." He stuffed his trash into the empty bag.

"I'm game, as long as you don't want to go kayaking or anything like that."

"When does the cast come off?" He glanced at her arm as he reached for the ignition.

"Maybe Monday. Maybe not. The doctor sounded like it was iffy. Pray for me. I don't want to be sidelined longer than necessary."

"No, but you don't want to go back to work too soon, either." As he threw the transmission into gear, his phone rang. He shoved the gearshift back into park and answered it. "Yeah? Okay." His dark eyes flitted to meet her gaze and he frowned. "Yeah, I'll be there as quick as I can." He clicked the phone off.

"Emergency?" Caddie asked.

"Afraid so. A charter boat needs help off Raspberry Island. I'm supposed to report to our sister ship, the *Shatney*. Half her crew's on leave, so any of the *Milroy*'s men who can get there fast will go out on the *Shatney*. I'm sorry."

Caddie lifted her right hand and raised her brows. "You can't help it."

"They've sent out a smaller boat already, but they may need us. I'll drop you at your apartment. It's almost on my way." Aven's shoulders drooped as he backed out of the parking space.

"We can go to the old fort some other day," she said.

"I'll take you up on that. Tomorrow, if we're back in time."

"Sure. Or the next day. Whatever works."

"I'll call you as soon as we're in, if it's not too late."

When he pulled up before her housing unit, Caddie reached for the door latch. "Don't get out. I can fend for myself."

"You sure? Your arm. . ."

On impulse, she leaned over and kissed him on the cheek. "I'm sure. I'll be praying for you and the people on the charter boat."

"Thanks."

His reaction was a little slow, but the last thing she saw as she slid down from the truck cab was his smile.

six

Aven arrived back at his apartment early the next morning. *Too early to call Caddie,* he reflected after consulting his watch. Robyn and Mom were probably up, fixing the dogs' rations, but he wouldn't hazard a guess as to whether Caddie would be awake at 0530 when she didn't have to report for duty. And if she was sleeping, he didn't want to wake her. She needed rest to help that arm heal.

After a quick snack, he called his sister instead.

Robyn answered and assured him that the family was getting along all right. "Grandpa's losing steam physically, but you knew that."

"Is his arthritis worse?"

"No, about the same as when you were here last. But he isn't able to do much of anything outside now. Mom's taken over all the chores he used to do and is taking care of him. I've had to pretty much run the business by myself the last few weeks."

"I'm sorry." Aven leaned on the card table he used as a kitchen table. He ought to be home, helping Mom and Robyn.

"It's not your fault. And, hey, I hitched my team up in the new harness yesterday. It was the first chance I'd had. I wanted to make sure it fit them right, and we did a ten-mile training run."

"Everything go okay?"

"They did great. I have a super team this year, Ave. I hope I can afford to take them in at least one race this winter."

"Too bad you can't run in ours."

"You know I can't run them in the Fire and Ice. We're the hosts. Duh! Besides, I'll be too busy. But I sure would like to do a short race, say in December. Or right after ours."

"Maybe you can. Wait and see how things go."

"I haven't given up on it."

"Are you and Mom going to be able to handle all the race preparations if Grandpa can't help you?" he asked. "That's a big job."

"It'll be tough, but I think it's worth it. We usually do a little better than break even, and it's our best advertisement. People come for the race and look over our kennels. I show my team off a little. Word of mouth is crucial in this business."

Aven wished he could take Caddie home to meet his family. It would be terrific if they could both get leave the week of the Fire and Ice and spend it in Wasilla, helping set up for the race.

"Hey, Rob, what would you think of me bringing a girl home sometime?"

"What?" Her shriek nearly pierced his eardrum. He held the phone away from his ear and cringed. "Did you say girl, as in female, young woman, dare I add love interest?"

She seemed to have come to a standstill, so he gingerly put the phone back to his ear. "Uh. . .yeah, I guess you could say any one of the above."

"Who is she? Is she Coast Guard? Or a townie? Tell me she's not someone you arrested."

Aven chuckled. "No way. She's a BM3. Stationed here. Serves on another ship."

"Oh, wow. That's perfect. She's a pay grade behind you. You can socialize, but she doesn't outrank you. Ave, that's fantastic. I want to meet her. When can you bring her? Can I tell Mom and Grandpa?"

"Slow down!" Aven couldn't stop grinning. "Yeah, I guess

you can tell them. Don't make too big a deal of it yet, though, okay? We've only gone out a couple of times. I like her a lot, but things are still in the early stages."

"So tell me everything."

"Naw, I don't think so."

"Is she pretty?"

"Yes. And smart."

"Ha! I figured that. You wouldn't like her if she weren't. Is she a Christian?"

"Definitely."

Robyn sighed. "I'm so happy that you've found someone."

"Well, like I said, it's not officially. . .anything. . .yet. I wanted to tell you so you wouldn't be shocked later on, if it works out. But if it doesn't. . ."

"You always amaze me."

That didn't seem to fit the conversation, or at least not the direction he'd been steering it, and Aven scowled. "How do you mean?"

"You're so sure of yourself when you're working. You're comfortable with yourself physically. Spiritually, too, I think. But when the emotions enter the picture, you hem and haw and won't commit to a ray of hope, let alone a long-term relationship."

"What do you know about it? You're no closer to finding a husband than I am a wife. Further away by a long shot, I'd say."

"And I'm four years younger than you are." Robyn chuckled. "Besides, I don't tell you everything."

Aven picked up on her teasing tone. "Oh? Something I should know?"

"Not really, but when there is I'll tell you."

"Okay. And if things progress with Caddie, I'll keep you posted."

"Caddie? Her name is Caddie? Like a golf minion?"

Aven choked on a laugh. "Her real name is Clarissa, but that's her nickname, okay? I've never seen her carrying a golf bag."

"Got it. Sounds to me like you'd better latch on to her fast. Nice girls are hard to come by in Alaska, you know."

"Watch it!"

"What's her last name?" Robyn asked with a chuckle.

"You want a lot, don't you? It's Lyle."

"Lyle?"

"That's right."

"Why is that name familiar?"

"I don't know."

After a couple of seconds' silence, Robyn said, "Oh, that captain."

"Huh?"

"You know. The man who tried to save Daddy and Jim Haskell."

Aven's stomach dropped.

"That was the man's name, remember?" Robyn persisted. "The one who died in Puget Sound when Daddy's plane crashed."

Aven found it hard to breathe past the huge lump in his throat. "You're right. That was his name." How could he not have realized? Caddie had told him that her father was stationed in Seattle at the time of his death. He could only conclude that he'd been so distracted by his feelings for her that he'd allowed his brain to take an unscheduled furlough.

"Aven?"

"Yeah?"

"We love you. Come home again soon."

"I will if I can."

"And bring the Caddie girl."

He hung up with a smile, imagining Caddie, in uniform, holding a golf club out to her captain. Nope. He liked the mental image of her in the green dress she'd worn to church last month far better.

He sobered as he mulled over his conversation with Robyn about Caddie's father. It had to be the same man. But did that matter? Caddie obviously didn't know. Would it disturb her if she found out? He tried to imagine how he would feel if their roles were reversed. Not good.

He checked the time. Still too early to call her. He ought to catch a nap, but he doubted he could sleep now. He still wanted to see Caddie if at all possible. Maybe they could explore Fort Abercrombie together. But should he reopen the subject of her father? His chest ached as he sat staring at the phone.

This was a matter for serious prayer.

❧

Caddie adjusted the focus on her camera and held her breath. She never would have dared get so close to bears in the wild on her own. But Aven had known where to find them and had driven close enough for her to get some great shots with her telephoto lens.

A mother brown bear scooped fish from the stream below them and tossed them to her cub on the bank, not seeming to notice the humans watching her. The youngster batted at the twitching fish. When the mother had supplied enough to satisfy her, the huge animals began to feed, ignoring the distant audience.

The stream gushed down a steep, green hillside toward the bay below. Caddie had never been to this part of Kodiak Island before. They had driven through rugged mountains but were only fifteen miles from the base. They'd passed Lake Buskin and navigated forest-covered slopes to come out on the northeast end of the island. The brilliant colors of spruce trees, grass, sky, and water thrilled her. In the distance, she glimpsed Whale Island and mountains all around the bay.

Aven had brought binoculars and continually swept the

vista before them while Caddie concentrated on the bears. She'd be glad when the nuisance cast came off her arm. Two more days, maybe. Monday couldn't come soon enough for her. But she wouldn't let that affect her outing today. Even with the unwieldy plaster accessory, she was able to handle the camera and zoom in on the bears. Mira and Jordan would love them. After the animals enjoyed their feast, they lumbered into the brush.

She sighed and turned back toward the pickup. "What are you looking for?" she asked Aven.

He lowered his binoculars. "Remember the man I told you about—Spruce Waller?"

"The one who hit you."

Aven winced.

"Sorry." Caddie put her camera carefully into its case. "What about him?"

"That's Anton Larsen Bay down there. We're not far from his place."

"Here? There's no town."

"No, there's not." Aven swept the air with his arm, indicating the hillsides and the inlet below. "There are some cabins. You can't see most of them from up here. But I thought I might be able to spot a boat in the harbor."

"And?"

"Nothing."

No, not nothing. He had hoped to find evidence relating to the cases his ship's crew had recently worked on. She went to stand beside him. "Can you drive all the way down to the shore on this side?"

"I think so."

They stood in silence for a long time. Caddie knew the meager roads on the island led to only a few of the nearest villages. Those farther away—like Larsen Bay, Old Harbor, and Akhiok—could only be reached by boat or by air.

"You brought me here in hopes of seeing Spruce Waller, didn't you?" she asked softly.

He cocked his head to one side. "Okay, I admit I went by his apartment in Kodiak. He wasn't around. I figured he might be out here."

"Or off on his brother's boat," Caddie hazarded.

"Well. . .the state police tried to contact his brother, but he wasn't home and his wife said she hadn't seen him in three days. Not that I believe that, but he could be over here with Spruce, lying low until the cops ease up on him."

"You hope you can link Spruce to the smuggling his brother is involved in, don't you?"

Aven shrugged. "So far, that's just a rumor. But I have to admit, that might ease the pain of seeing our ship get staved up."

"And getting jumped by half a dozen fishermen?"

He bit his bottom lip. After a long moment of silence, he turned toward her. "I guess I should have told you what was on my mind before I drove out here."

"I don't mind being here. In fact, I'd love it if we could find the guy who owns the boat."

"Clay Waller."

"Whoever. But I don't want to mix things up with a couple of tough guys. My arm's still in the cast. I wouldn't be any help in a fight."

"I'm sorry, Caddie. You're absolutely right. Coming out here was foolish of me, and not asking you was selfish."

She reached up and touched his cheek. "I'm not trying to lay guilt on you. I'm just saying we should be careful." She looked down toward the bay. "Want to see how close we can drive to the shore?"

He hesitated. "It would probably be smarter to just forget it."

She watched his face until he raised the binoculars again. "We could hike on down there," she said.

"No. Too many bears around. All I brought for insurance is my pistol. We don't want to get too far from the truck."

"Then let's drive on a ways."

"You sure?"

"Yes. But if we find Waller, we don't approach him."

After half a minute of staring through the binoculars, he lowered them and faced her. "Deal. I'll be careful."

They got into the truck, and he drove another half mile. Aven's broody silence dragged Caddie's spirits down. Were the Waller brothers affecting him this badly? Or was there something else he hadn't told her?

When they came to a wide spot almost to the bay, he pulled over. "I don't want to get where they can see us. I'll turn around so we're headed out, and then we'll take a look-see." Aven maneuvered the truck into a better position, grabbed his binoculars from the seat, and climbed out of the cab.

Caddie opened her door and followed him, once more carrying her camera.

He stood off the edge of the road, scanning the terrain and water below them. "There's a boat docked down there."

"Where?" Caddie strained to see where he was looking. "Is that a roofline?"

"Yes. The cabin's above the water fifty yards or so, and the boat's moored down below. Come on." He plunged into the brush beside the road.

What about bears? Caddie glanced uneasily around and hurried to catch up with him.

Aven stopped inside the tree line beside a log cabin. He parted the branches of a clump of alders and again peered through his field glasses.

The sun glittered on the placid water of a cove below. Movement drew Caddie's attention, and she sucked in a breath. "Is that the boat you chased?"

Aven let out a sigh. "Hard to be sure. They had a canopy

on when we saw it, and it had a dark stripe just below the gunwales, but. . ."

"But they're painting it." Caddie squinted and focused on the two men below them. "Do you think they would change the registration number?"

Aven rubbed the back of his neck and adjusted the strap on his binoculars. "People do it all the time with cars. Put on false license plates. Why not with a boat if they don't want it identified easily? They've painted over the name for sure."

"So they rename the boat, maybe change a couple of the numbers, and alter the appearance the best they can—maybe add something on deck to change the silhouette or put a different color canopy on top."

"Right, so that we can't be sure it's the same boat at a glance." Aven frowned. "I'd like to get closer."

"Do you think that's wise?" Caddie's pulse accelerated. Facing lawbreakers while in uniform may be part of her job, but out here, with only the waves for witnesses?

"Probably not," Aven said. "Wish I could see their faces." Again he studied the scene below.

"Would you recognize Spruce Waller?"

"Absolutely, if I could get within five yards of him. But I've never seen his brother that I know of." He pulled the binoculars from his face with a frustrated sigh. "The guy on the left has the same build as Spruce, but I can't be sure from here that it's him. It could be his brother or someone else entirely." He eyed the nearby cabin and looked again toward the small dock and the moored boat.

"Think what could happen if they saw us. I mean. . . that guy tried to kill you." Caddie clamped her lips shut, determined to say no more. Her heart thudded.

Aven said nothing but peered toward the boat again.

Caddie lifted her camera and focused on the man wielding the paintbrush. At that moment he straightened, and even from her distant vantage point, she could see that he was a large, muscular man.

"He's growing his beard out," Aven said.

As the man turned to speak to his companion, Caddie clicked a photo.

"I think I got a decent shot," she whispered. "We can enlarge it on the computer."

"Great." Suddenly Aven let his binoculars drop on their strap and grabbed her wrist, tugging her downward. "He's looking up here."

She turned her face away and whipped her silver-toned camera behind her then crouched still behind the shrubs. After a long moment, she hissed, "Think he saw us?"

"No. But it's a good thing we stayed behind the bushes."

She exhaled. "Maybe we'd better leave before he looks again."

Aven moved stealthily through the trees, and Caddie followed. They halted out of sight of the boat but farther from the pickup.

"There's a vehicle parked on the other side of the cabin," Aven said softly. "I'd like to get the plate number so we can be sure we've got the right man."

Caddie shivered. "Take my camera and get a picture."

"Good idea."

She handed it to him.

"Wait here," he said.

"Okay, but don't take any chances."

He darted in a crouch to the back corner of the building. For a minute and a half, he was out of sight. Caddie held her breath, listening and watching the spot where he'd disappeared.

At last he returned, racing almost silently toward her. "Got it." He seized Caddie's hand. "Let's get out of here."

seven

Playing Scrabble with the Phifers Monday evening kept Caddie calm, so long as she didn't think about Aven and their Saturday expedition to Anton Larsen Bay.

They'd spent a quiet Sunday on the base, but Aven had fidgeted all day, biding his time until he could contact his commanding officer.

"You'll hear from Aven soon," Jo-Lynn said, and Caddie realized she'd checked her watch again.

"Sorry. I didn't expect him to be gone all day."

Mark reached across the kitchen table for game tiles to replace his stock of letters. "They probably went to talk to the state police. Sometimes things like that take way longer than they should."

Caddie nodded. She hoped Aven hadn't involved himself in another confrontation with the bullheaded Spruce Waller.

Her cell phone trilled at five minutes after seven o'clock, and adrenaline sent her pulse rocketing.

"Hi. I wondered if I could bring your camera back to you," Aven said.

Caddie relaxed and smiled across the kitchen table at Jo-Lynn. "Sure, but I'm not home. I'm over at Mark and Jo-Lynn's."

"Okay, I'll come there."

"Is that Aven?" Jo-Lynn jumped up. "Ask him if he ate supper."

"Have you eaten?" Caddie asked. "Jo-Lynn has leftover lasagna."

"Sounds good. Tell her I'll be there in five."

Caddie clicked her phone off. "Thanks, Jo-Lynn. He's on his way."

"Aw, come on," Mark whined. "I've got a really good word. You're not going to quit the game, are you?"

With a laugh, Caddie looked to Jo-Lynn. "How about it?"

"Let me put a plate in the microwave for Aven and I'll come back."

A short time later, Aven ravenously attacked the food while the others finished their game.

"There," Mark crowed. "I used all my letters." He set out tiles to spell *brown* and prodded them into place with a fingertip. "I win."

"No, you don't." Jo-Lynn half rose, grabbing letter tiles from her own rack. "Caddie and I get one more turn, and I get double word score on *maw*, using your W."

"That's not a word."

"Yes, it is."

Mark scowled at her. "You're making that up. Do we have a dictionary?"

"It's a word," Aven said.

"I thought it was *Ma*, M-A."

Caddie laughed. "Maw is a different word. It means stomach, I think."

"Yeah." Jo-Lynn's eyes gleamed. "Like Aven is filling his maw with lasagna."

"Okay, I give up." Mark shook his head, glowering at the board.

Caddie said, "Cheer up, Mark. I still can't make any words, and I think you won after all." They'd given her the scorekeeper's job, and she quickly totted up the points. "Yup. Sorry, Jo-Lynn. He's got you by two points."

Jo-Lynn let out a sharp breath and stamped her foot. A moment later, however, she joined them all in laughter. "Okay, but I was close."

"You were, babe. Good match." Mark leaned over to kiss her.

Caddie shot a glance at Aven, and he winked at her. "Got any coffee, Jo-Lynn?"

Their hostess stood. "Sure. You want some, Caddie?"

"Yes, please."

"Mark?"

"Natch."

Jo-Lynn headed for the counter to measure the coffee.

"So, what did you find out?" Mark asked Aven. "Caddie told us you took her camera to the state police with pictures of some SUV you found out in the woods."

"That's not what I said." Caddie had learned by now that Mark was expert at teasing.

"Seriously, what happened?" Mark asked.

Aven laid down his fork and wiped his mouth on his napkin. "The skipper went with me, and we talked to the same state trooper I called after our cruise the other day. They sent two men out to Waller's cabin. Spruce Waller was there, but his brother wasn't. And the boat had disappeared."

"They moved it," Mark said.

"Yeah. I wish we could have gotten them to go out there Saturday night. Clay probably took the boat back to his place at the other end of the island. But the trooper wasn't in a hurry to rush out there again. He said he's got bigger fish to fry."

Caddie sighed. "I can understand that, since you didn't have any proof to begin with that they'd committed a crime. Other than not responding when your skipper hailed the boat, I mean."

"And you weren't even sure the second man working on the boat Saturday was the brother, were you?" Mark asked.

"Caddie's pictures say it was. The trooper ID'd Clay Waller from the photos."

"Even from so far away?" Caddie asked.

Aven nodded. "He said you did a great job with your telephoto."

Jo-Lynn brought them all mugs of coffee. "Well, quit looking so glum, all of you. The boys came home for an extra three days, and I'm not complaining."

"I'm not either," Mark told her, "but we have to report back to the ship tomorrow morning. What about you, Caddie?"

She pulled out a smile that she didn't feel. "I've been assigned to light duty on shore starting tomorrow."

Aven gazed at her over his coffee mug. "For how long?"

"I'm not sure. I saw the doctor again this afternoon. He thinks a couple of weeks. Then, if the cast is off the next time the *Wintergreen* goes out, I'll be aboard."

"Don't worry, Aven. I'll keep an eye on her." Jo-Lynn resumed her seat and smiled over at him. "Caddie and I can hang out while you guys are at sea."

"All right," Aven said, watching Caddie keenly. "I guess that's better than sitting around doing nothing."

"Watch it!" Jo-Lynn grabbed her spoon and drew her arm back as though about to attack him. "I may not be in uniform, but I do *not* 'do nothing' all day."

Aven laughed and turned to Caddie. "Let me drive you home?"

Caddie felt her face warm. "Thanks."

Mark's face clouded up in mock disgust. "She only lives two hundred feet away, for crying out loud."

"Yeah, and the sun will stay out until midnight," Jo-Lynn added.

"A lot can happen on a two-hundred-foot walk," Aven said sternly. "You just never know. I think she needs an escort." Under the table, his hand found Caddie's and he squeezed her fingers.

"Now that you mention it," she said, smiling at Jo-Lynn, "we should probably head out. The *Milroy*'s crew has to report early."

"Eh, we're used to it," Mark said.

"I think Caddie's right. We'd better skedaddle." Aven shoved back his chair. "Thanks for the lasagna."

The evening shone as bright as midday, and Caddie felt conspicuous as Aven walked her from his truck to her door a few minutes later. "Thanks for bringing my camera back."

He held the case out, and she took it with her good hand. "You're welcome. Thanks for getting those pictures. We saw your bear pictures, too. Couldn't help it, going through to retrieve the ones of the Wallers."

"That's okay."

Aven nodded. "Your shots of the bears are really good."

"Thanks."

"What are you going to do with them?"

"I don't know. Send copies to my brother and sister. Maybe make a Christmas card. I just like photographing wildlife." She held the camera against her side with her cast while fumbling in her pocket with her other hand for her door key.

"Well, I think you should sell them."

"What?" She jerked her chin up and stared into his eyes. "They can't be *that* good."

"Sure they can. They're every bit as good as the pictures they have in the tourist brochures."

"You think so?"

"Yeah. A lot of people would think so. It's a gift. My sister Robyn took about a thousand pictures of her dogs before she got any good enough to put on a brochure advertising the kennel and the sled race my family sponsors every year."

Caddie studied his face. The dark shadows under his

eyes reinforced his serious tone. "Thanks. A lot."

Aven reached for the key ring she held. "Let me open this for you."

She surrendered the ring, and he slid her door key into the lock. "There." He stooped toward her and brushed her lips with his.

A sense of joy and loss swept over Caddie. Aven would be out two weeks this time. What if she'd been deployed again when he returned? They could go on missing each other in port for months.

She wanted to put her arms around him and cling to him, but even if she dared, the stupid cast would prevent that. She looked up at him and tried to think of the appropriate words for this uncertain parting.

"Caddie. . ."

"Yes?"

His jaw muscles tightened. He looked away for a moment, inhaling deeply. When his gaze returned to hers, she sensed that he'd reached a decision.

"There's something I need to talk to you about."

"Besides the Waller brothers?"

"Yes."

"Okay." She tried to divine from his sober expression what it could be. Nothing good or he wouldn't carry that air of dread and reluctance. "Do you want to come in?"

He exhaled. "Thanks. I promise I won't stay long."

She opened the door and led him inside. "Have a seat." She settled on the sofa she'd inherited from the last tenants.

He sat beside her and leaned forward, clasping his hands between his knees.

She waited.

After a moment, he took a deep breath, but still said nothing.

"Aven, what is it?"

He jumped up and walked to the window, where he stood looking out at the parking area. "Look, there's something. . .it's nothing bad, really, but I figured I should tell you. If you found out from someone else. . ." He ran a hand through his dark hair. "Caddie, I wasn't trying to keep it from you."

Her stomach lurched. A dozen possibilities raced through her mind. He couldn't be married. Could he? Maybe he was being transferred out soon. Or perhaps he merely struggled with a way to let her down. But if that was the case, then why had he kissed her—sort of?

She stood and walked over to stand near him. "Please tell me what's wrong."

He turned and pulled his shoulders back. "It's about my father. I didn't realize it at first, but when I talked to Robyn, she made the connection. If it bothers you, I'm very sorry. I don't want to upset you. But I don't want to take this relationship any further until you know."

Know what? She blinked and pulled in a breath but couldn't say a word. Was his father a criminal?

Aven took her elbow gently and steered her back toward the couch. "Let's sit down."

She complied, shooting off a quick plea to heaven for serenity, no matter what. "Okay," she said when they were seated again. "There's something about your dad. You can tell me. Please."

He licked his lips and nodded. "Okay. See, when you told me your father was in the Coast Guard, I should have realized he was Captain Gregory Lyle. Wasn't he?"

"Yes, but. . ." She waited. There was more coming, of course.

"And he was stationed in Seattle three years ago, when he died."

"That's right. It's no secret."

"No, it's not. And he died in the line of duty."

She lowered her head. "Yes."

"Trying to rescue my father."

She jerked her head up and stared at him. As the pieces fit together in her mind, breathing became a chore. "Oh Aven, I'm so sorry. It was bad enough that we both. . ." She stopped and sniffed, thinking about their simultaneous grief, back before they knew each other. "You said the plane crashed. I didn't think about it being the same one. I figured you meant a commercial jet."

"No. it was a small private plane the oil company owned." Aven looked across the room at nothing. "Their pilot, Jim Haskell, was taking Dad to Seattle to catch a commercial flight to Houston. A storm warning was posted, but Jim figured they'd beat the weather. But when they got to Puget Sound, it came on suddenly and they went down in the storm. Jim managed to call for help before the plane sank, and the Coast Guard responded."

Caddie nodded. "My dad was on call. He and three other men went out in a rescue boat. They found a few pieces of the wreckage and were looking for survivors." She faltered and looked up at him, tears flooding her eyes and constricting her throat.

"It must have been awful weather," Aven said. "Your father was standing on the deck, and he got hit by lightning. That's what we were told."

"Yes. A freak accident."

"But if my dad wasn't out there. . . I mean, if he and Jim had listened to the weather predictions. . ."

Caddie eased back into the couch cushions, but they offered little comfort. Her chest hurt as she forced herself to look beyond the surface, to plunge past the natural reaction. She would not blame Aven, nor his father, though her natural inclination was to think—to say—that he had caused the death of another man by his foolishness.

"It's not your fault." She shuddered and closed her eyes for a moment, seeking strength she didn't feel. At last she was able to look at him again. "It's probably not even their fault. Weather patterns change quickly."

Aven sighed, and she could tell from the agitation in his dark eyes that he'd seen her struggle. "I thought about not saying anything, but I couldn't let you hear something and put two and two together. Caddie, I wish it had happened differently."

"Me, too." *Or not at all.* How many times had she cried out to God for understanding? Why her father? Why lightning? After all his years in the Coast Guard, with all his experience on stormy seas, why was Gregory Lyle the one to die that way? And now, to learn that Aven's father had—

She caught herself. She wouldn't even think that Aven's father was to blame. It would be too easy to let something like that fester and spread into a chronic bitterness. Her tears overflowed and a sob erupted from her chest.

Aven folded her in his arms and drew her close. "I'm sorry. I'm so sorry."

She heard the tears in his thick voice. They sat together for what seemed like a long time. She couldn't reconcile the warmth of his embrace with the sharp pain inside her. He began rubbing slow circles on her back with his sturdy palm, and she wilted against his chest, gulping to control her weeping.

After a long time, she sat up and wiped her eyes. "I'm sorry. I didn't mean to lose it like that."

"It's my fault," he said. "There must have been a better way to tell you."

"No. I'm glad you let me know now. You're right about that. It would have been harder later. But. . .I'm not upset with you. You hear me?" She leaned back and looked up into his glistening eyes, willing herself to believe it, too.

He nodded. "Yeah. I still feel bad about not catching on sooner and having to dump it on you, so to speak."

"Quit that." She tried to scowl, but the tears were too recent, so she sniffed and patted his chest softly. "It's going to be okay."

"If you're sure. . ." He studied her for a long moment. "I should probably leave now."

She supposed he had been there long enough, but she hated to see him go. "I'll see you. . ." *When?*

He reached up and caught one of her straggling tears and let his fingers linger gently on her cheek. "Yeah. Soon, I hope. I'll be praying for you."

"Watch yourself." She straightened and inhaled, determined to end this without crying again, even if they wouldn't see each other again for who knew how long. Knowing she would miss him tangled inextricably with her apprehension about resuming her duties and her turmoil over her own feelings for her father. She determined not to drift into another emotional maelstrom.

She reached over to touch his sleeve. "If you meet up with the Waller brothers, be careful. Not that you wouldn't be anyway, but. . .oh, you know what I mean."

"I think I do. *Semper paratus.*"

She nodded. *Always ready,* the Coast Guard's motto. She'd been far from ready for his revelation. Would she be ready when the time came for her to serve again on the *Wintergreen*? "You'll do great," she said. "I'll pray for you, too."

Aven slid his arm around her, drawing her closer, and bent to kiss her with more confidence than he'd shown at the door.

She leaned against him for one more warm moment, relishing his strength and solidity. Then she pulled away with a sigh. Prolonging the farewell would have her in tears again.

"Come on," she said.

When she stood, he rose and followed her to the door. He hesitated there.

She smiled up at him.

"No bad feelings? About our dads, that is?" he asked.

She managed a smile. "I can't see any room for guilt in our generation."

He sighed and stroked her hair. "Thanks." He opened the door and went out into the too-bright evening.

eight

Three weeks later, Aven's ship docked in Seward to pick up an officer and leave supplies. He'd hoped the *Milroy* would return to Kodiak before Caddie's ship embarked again, but it looked like he'd just miss her. She was due to deploy at high tide the next morning, several hours before he would arrive in port.

He'd found the past few weeks frustrating, though he'd kept too busy to be bored. The days blurred into a haze until he felt that July had skipped over him somehow and August had arrived without fanfare. Five days into the month, the long Arctic days had noticeably shortened. The wind had a nip of autumn. Summer was a fleeting patch of sea smoke, already dissipating.

Tomorrow Caddie would at last go back on active duty. Aven had seen her only twice since the evening when he'd kissed her, and both events left him longing for more time with her. He'd managed to make a church service with her the first time, and on the second occasion, he and Caddie met for a quick cup of coffee on the base during her break from office work. It was unsatisfactory, though he'd received a few erratic e-mails when he was able to check his account. Each time, he'd replied with assurances that her notes encouraged him. But real time—face time—with Caddie was hard to come by.

He called her cell phone from Seward, where his skipper had logged them in for the night. At least he could get phone service here, which he couldn't for the most part on the sea.

"I'm so glad you called." Her voice held an air of

confession. He'd learned her moods well enough to read doubts, dread, and lack of confidence in her choppy breathing.

"Tomorrow's the big day, huh?"

"Yes. I don't know what's wrong with me. The cast is off, my arm feels fine, and I'm going back to active duty. Yay."

Aven grimaced. "What's up really?"

She hesitated. "Nerves, I think. I don't know when this happened, but I'm scared to go back."

"Scared you won't do well?"

"Yes. And that I won't be able to pull my weight. I'm still not back to full strength. And then there's always Boatswain Tilley."

"I know him. He can be tough on petty officers."

"I can take tough. But if he goes on to humiliation, I'm not so sure. I guess the thought of going back has worried me more than I realized. Add to that the fact that I'll see you even less when we're both in and out of port, and I'm afraid I've let myself wallow in self-pity."

"I've been thinking about you all day."

"Thanks." Her voice held genuine warmth this time.

He smiled, glad he'd had the power to cheer her even a little bit. "Praying for you, too."

"I really need it. Aven, I can't imagine not having you there to give me a boost when I'm down."

"It works both ways. You pick me up just by letting me care about you." He glanced around to make sure no one stood close enough to hear him sweet-talking her. His shipmates would razz him for sure if they knew he was getting serious about a woman. But he meant every word.

"Thanks so much," she said.

"I wish I could see you tonight, but I can't. So just know that I'm thinking of you. I miss you, but I know sooner or later we'll get some time together, if it's in God's plan for us."

"I like that thought. I'm going to hold on to it." She definitely sounded more upbeat now.

His heart seemed about to melt, and he wished more than ever that he could see her. Squeeze her hand. Give her a hug.

"I'll miss you," she said. "But I feel a lot better because you called."

"I'm glad. And we will see each other again. Soon."

&

One short week later, Caddie stood between two seamen, watching as the ship's crane lowered a huge buoy to rest on the deck. She gave it a quick visual inspection and found it in good enough repair to stay out another year. Her team of five men would go over it thoroughly to be sure. They scurried to secure it in place, before the rollicking waves could shift the buoy and endanger the crew. She tried not to think of her last sea voyage and the injured arm that still ached in damp weather.

When the buoy was safely chained down, Caddie signaled the crane operator and instructed two of her men to check the mooring chain. Others prepared to change the lamp bulbs and repaint the buoy with special, quick-drying paint. In less than an hour, they should have it back in the water.

"What's that?" Seaman Morales asked.

She walked around to stand beside him. A yellow plastic streamer fluttered from the steel lifting eye at the top of the buoy. "You got me."

"Maybe someone used the buoy as a marker in a regatta," Morales suggested.

If so, it had been a very low-profile regatta. The Coast Guard was usually notified of boat races and other sporting events on the water. Frowning, Caddie gave the streamer a yank and broke it off. She handed it to Morales. "Trash."

He nodded and carried it away.

She circled the buoy, observing the seamen's labor. All worked with concentration that told her they were determined to make the paint job perfect.

As she watched them, her thoughts drifted to Aven. She'd received only one message from him since their last phone call—a brief e-mail. Even though he'd kept the tone general, his words had lifted her spirits.

> *Caddie, I'm in port. Going out again tomorrow.*
> *Hope things are going well for you. Psalm 93. BM2 A.*
> *Holland.*

She'd printed out the message on the bridge yesterday and tucked it in her pocket to savor later. In the tiny cabin she shared with Lindsey, she'd looked up the Psalm and read it slowly several times. Even though the Hebrew poem had been translated into English, it rang with splendor.

> *"The LORD reigns, he is robed in majesty; the LORD is*
> *robed in majesty and is armed with strength. . . .*
> *The seas have lifted up, O LORD, the seas have lifted*
> *up their voice; the seas have lifted up their pounding*
> *waves. Mightier than the thunder of the great waters,*
> *mightier than the breakers of the sea—the LORD on*
> *high is mighty."*

The verses fit her life so exactly that she closed her eyes and whispered, "Thank You for showing me this, Lord."

Now, as she stood on deck, the words came back to her. She felt like shouting them aloud for all the sailors to hear, but she kept quiet. Wouldn't Boatswain Tilley love it if she lost her head and started spouting scripture while her crew halted their work to stare at her?

She focused her attention on the job at hand. Refitting this buoy was the crew's last official task on this trip, and when it was over, they would head for Kodiak. The remote possibility that she would see Aven within the next few days considerably lightened her mood.

When the men had finished their work, she handed one of them her clipboard. "Perform the checklist and make sure this buoy is in top condition, Daley."

"Aye, aye, Petty Officer Lyle."

She held back a smile as the earnest young man began the new task. Daley was close to testing for a pay grade increase, and she'd been advised to give him more responsibility.

When he'd finished running down the checklist, he handed the clipboard back to her. "All set, ma'am."

"Don't call me ma'am," she said softly. He nodded. "All right then, Daley. I'll check our position." As buoy deck supervisor, she calculated their position herself, ensuring that the navigational aid would be returned to the right place in the water so sailors could trust it to keep them from straying into the shallows. "Men, take your positions to release the chain stoppers. Daley, signal the crane operator."

Daley gave the command, and the crane lifted the buoy again and swung it toward the side of the ship.

Caddie held her breath as she watched. That thing weighed as much as a small car, and the crew exercised great respect for airborne objects of that magnitude, standing well back in case anything went wrong and the buoy unexpectedly crashed to the deck.

It was nearly to the rail when a rogue wave caught the ship, interrupting its regular pitch and roll, tilting them sideways. Everyone grabbed the nearest stable object.

Caddie was near the lifeboat rack and braced herself against it. When the ship rolled back, the mammoth buoy swayed like a pendulum toward the rising rail.

"Watch it," Caddie called to her men. She turned and looked up at the crane operator. "Come on," she said under her breath. "Higher. Get that thing over the side."

Wind whipped her hair, and the deck slanted drastically beneath her feet. Behind her, a shout preceded a loud *thunk*. The deck shuddered. Caddie whirled. Men were scrambling as the buoy shivered in midair then swung out over the waves.

The ship shifted with the next swell. To her relief, the deck came back to near level. The huge buoy had cleared the rail and hung well over the side. The crane operator quickly extended the cable and lowered the buoy to the water.

She exhaled as her men rushed to the rail to watch.

"What's the damage?"

Caddie jumped. Boatswain Tilley, via radio, had spoken rather curtly in her ear. She swallowed hard and turned to look up at the forecastle. "I'll make an inspection, sir."

"No one hurt?"

"Negative." She did a quick mental count of her team, realizing she hadn't actually had time to find out but had spoken quickly to protect them and herself from Tilley's wrath. She strode to the rail trying not to appear in too big a hurry and addressed Daley. "Everyone okay?"

"Yes, ma'am. Petty Officer."

Caddie peered down at the buoy, which bobbed in the foaming water. She said into her radio, "Buoy in place. Over."

"The boatswain has left the fo'cas'l," a seaman replied. "He'll be on deck in a second."

Caddie gulped. If she hadn't guessed anyone else was listening, she'd have thanked him for the warning.

She ordered the men to clean up the deck.

They dashed about collecting scattered tools.

"Lyle."

Caddie managed not to flinch and turned to greet the boatswain. "Boatswain Tilley?"

"Was there any damage when that buoy hit the bulwark?"

"I don't believe so. There's a small dent in the rail. Some paint chipped off. Barely visible."

"Show me."

She straightened her shoulders and marched beside him to the where the collision had occurred. "Right there."

Tilley scowled. "Have your men repaint this section of the rail. And when you dismiss your detail, you'll stand an extra watch, Lyle."

Anger boiled up inside her, but she quickly shoved it down and lowered her gaze. "Aye, aye."

"And the crane operator and the man directing him will report to the galley."

She glanced up at him then away. It wouldn't do any good to protest, though the men were not at fault. At least the buoy hadn't hit anyone or anything fragile. "Aye, aye."

Tilley turned on his heel and left the deck.

Caddie stood still for several seconds, calming herself and praying silently before she faced the tasks of dismissing the men and sending Daley and Ricker to KP duty. It wasn't fair. She hated taking the men's recreation time away from them. They'd done nothing to deserve it.

She didn't mind the extra duty for herself, though Tilley shouldn't have given her such an assignment. He wasn't her commanding officer. She wouldn't protest, though. Even if she had the chance to have the order rescinded, she didn't want to deepen Tilley's dislike of her. Another four hours on duty wouldn't hurt her, and accepting his disrespect might even help her to learn patience and submission. Still, she was tired and her arm had begun to ache.

She called her team to attention and gave orders for the

small repair job. "Daley. Ricker. When you are dismissed, you will report to the chef in the galley and do whatever he instructs you to do." She didn't meet the men's eyes. If she smiled, grimaced, she would betray the emotion swirling through her. She mustn't give Tilley ammunition. He would accuse her of being soft or disrespectful—or any one of a number of adjectives she'd never considered. "You are dismissed."

She felt very alone as she watched the men leave the deck.

nine

"I can't believe we both have this afternoon free." Aven set their golf bags down near the first tee of Bear Valley, the nine-hole golf course near the base.

Caddie's blue eyes shone as she gathered her things. "Me either. Thanks so much for thinking of this."

"Are you sure your arm can take it?"

"Pretty sure, but if it starts aching, I'll let you know."

"Good." Aven handed her a golf ball.

When he'd learned Caddie's ship would dock in time to allow them half a day together, he'd considered a kayaking venture. That probably would be bad for her arm, though. He wouldn't want to do anything to set her recovery back. He'd held back from asking her at first, for fear she might carry some nebulous resentment for his father's role in her own dad's death. But she'd gotten past that, and he appreciated that proof of her maturity.

"I'm really lousy at golf, in spite of my name," she said with a laugh.

He chuckled, recalling Robyn's comments about Caddie's name. "Me, too." He hesitated and decided to come clean. "Okay, I've only played on a golf course once, and that was here. I did so horribly I never came back."

"Sounds like we'll be evenly matched. And we'd better let anyone behind us play through."

Caddie set up her first ball and teed off.

Aven shielded his eyes and followed the ball's path. "Not bad. I guess." He grinned at her. "Actually, I'm not sure if that's good or not."

"Could have been worse, I guess." She flexed her left arm and smiled at him. "My arm feels fine so far. If I'm sore tomorrow, it'll be because I used my muscles more than usual, not because of the injury. That's pretty well healed now."

"I'm glad." He stooped to set his ball on the tee. "Now that the sun's getting lower, the breeze off the bay feels chilly for August."

"Yes, I'm glad I wore my vest today." Caddie stood back a little and waited for him to swing.

Just knowing she was watching made him nervous, and he completely missed the ball on his first try. "Oops." He took a deep breath and concentrated. The second swing was a little better, sending the ball flying up the fairway nearly as far as Caddie's had gone. Aven exhaled in relief. Maybe he should have chosen something he knew more about.

They blundered their way through the nine holes. Caddie kept him laughing, and in the end their scores were fairly even.

After they returned their equipment to the clubhouse, Aven tried to think of a way to prolong the interlude together. "How about a soda in the snack bar?"

Caddie glanced into the crowded shop. "There are a lot of people in there. What if we got drinks and took them outside?"

Aven bought two bottled soft drinks, and they hurried outside. They found a bench in the sun, and she seemed content to sit there with him, around the corner of the clubhouse where they couldn't be seen from the parking lot.

Aven slid close to her and rested his arm on the back of the bench behind her. "Warm enough?" he asked.

"Yes."

The breeze ruffled her hair and shot golden highlights through it.

"So, how did your cruise go? Everything all right?"

"Pretty much," she said. "How about you? You didn't say much about your last deployment. Any arrests this time?"

"No." He sipped his soda and inched closer to her, bringing his arm down around her shoulders.

She smiled without looking at him.

He felt comfortable, not awkward, with her now and was thankful for the milestones they'd passed. "We gave quite a few citations, but we didn't have to impound any boats or haul anyone in."

"Good. Hey, I didn't tell you about my grandmother's newspaper."

"No, I can't say that you have. Your grandmother has a newspaper?"

She chuckled. "No, she subscribes to one. She lives in Oregon, and she wrote and told me that they run a travel feature every Sunday. She suggested I write an article about Kodiak Island and send it to her paper."

"Are you going to?"

"Thinking about it."

Aven nodded, picturing Caddie's photos splashed across the page and her name in the byline. "Be sure to send a few of your bear pictures."

"Definitely. And I thought maybe I'd call a few of the charter boat owners and the people who have tourist lodges."

"Yeah, that'd make a great layout." He looked out over the brilliant green before him. At last Caddie was right where he'd yearned to have her. For weeks he'd longed to be with her, to hold her in his arms, and to have the chance for another serious, in-person talk with her. This was more than he'd hoped for. He sent up a silent prayer of gratitude.

She leaned away from him a little, and he felt a cool breeze cut between them.

"I wasn't entirely honest a minute ago." She frowned and met his gaze. "It's true nothing major happened on my deployment, but even so, I don't feel good about it."

"Why not?"

She shrugged. "Maybe I was away from the job too long. It seemed as though some of my shipmates felt I'd let them down."

"It's not like you were slacking. You broke your arm."

"I know. But. . .we were just getting to work as a real team and I left for a month. And things that bothered me before seemed worse this time. Like Tilley. I've felt from the start as though he was watching me, looking for something to criticize. It was worse than ever this time. Maybe he thinks it was my fault that I got hurt. And what about this—maybe it was."

"It couldn't have been. You were out there doing everything you could to save those fishermen. You didn't do anything stupid or negligent. The sea got you. That's all." Aven drew her gently back into the circle of his arm.

Caddie let him, and she nestled in against his sweatshirt, resting her head just below his collarbone. "Thanks."

He gave her a little squeeze. "All right. Aside from Tilley and feeling inadequate, how did it go?"

She sighed, and he wondered what thoughts plagued her. He sat still, waiting without speaking, stroking her shoulder gently.

After a couple of minutes, she pulled in a deep breath. "When I joined the Coast Guard, I thought this would be my life. Twenty or thirty years anyway."

"And now?" he asked.

"Now I'm not so sure. Since Dad died, I've had these doubts as to whether I really belong here. Did I join because I wanted to sail and have adventures? To serve my country? Or to make Dad happy? I'm doing well at the job, I think— that is, I was until I broke my arm—but now I wonder if I was wrong. Did I make a mistake going into the service?"

"No."

"No? Just like that?" She pushed away from him and studied his face.

Aven smiled. "Everybody goes through this. It's natural. You start second-guessing yourself, wondering if you've overlooked something major. It usually happens right before a test or a transfer."

"Think so?"

"Know so."

"I am studying for my next test."

"See? That'll do it."

She settled back in, and he rested his cheek against the top of her head. She snuggled closer against his side, and Aven closed his eyes for a few seconds. For that moment, he wished they were both far away from Kodiak, free from their military obligations. But only for a moment.

"You know how you mentioned the motto a few weeks back?" she asked.

"Semper paratus."

"Yes. Always ready. Well, I don't feel ready."

"For the physical strain?"

"No. It's more mental and emotional." She raised her head and looked fiercely at him. "We had a minor incident. The seas were rough and a buoy we were hoisting hit the ship's rail, but nobody was injured and none of the equipment was hurt. Tilley punished me and two others."

Aven frowned. "Some people do that. Was he hard on you?"

"No, not really, but it made me angry. With Tilley. He's a bully."

"He's a boatswain. It's part of his job to keep things running smoothly."

She shook her head. "This wouldn't help things run better. Those men did nothing wrong, and he had to know it.

That wave that rocked us was a fluke."

"What did he do to you?"

She shrugged. "An extra shift. It wasn't that bad, and I managed to control my reaction. But it made me furious inside, and then it made me sad and depressed."

"Did you pray about it?"

"I tried. It didn't seem to help mend my attitude."

They sat still for a long time, until Aven stirred. "I don't have all the answers, but sometimes things happen in the service that we don't think are right."

"Oh, I know. This wasn't all that important. That's part of what worries me. Why am I making it such a big deal? Because Tilley made a big deal out of a small incident?"

"Maybe. But you need to keep your focus where it belongs. No matter what happens—no matter if your CO is a nutcase, or if you lose a man overboard, or if your paycheck gets lost on its way to your bank account—you have to remember that God's in charge. As far as God is concerned, I figure I'm still in recruit training."

Caddie tilted her head to one side. "I suppose so. I know I have a long way to go."

"We all do. But when I think of our motto, I don't just think of being ready to fulfill my duties or being ready to help people in trouble. I think about being ready for whatever God brings my way."

She let her shoulders slump and shook her head a little. "You make it sound easy."

"Sorry. It's not. It's easy to say but hard to do on a consistent basis."

"So, you don't think I made a mistake when I enlisted?"

"No. That's what you felt God called you to do at the time."

Her blue eyes glistened, and he wondered if she was on the verge of tears. Her voice cracked when she spoke again.

"Does God change His mind?"

"No, but He might change yours."

She swung her half-empty bottle of cola through the air in a gesture of frustration. "But I was so sure!"

Aven shifted on the bench to face her squarely. "With me it's the opposite. I joined the Coast Guard mostly as a way to finance my education. After I got in, I found out I loved it. This is my education and career rolled into one. I just didn't know it eight years ago."

Caddie leaned back against the bench, and Aven ran his fingers over the back of her vest, between her shoulder blades. She nodded slowly. "I'm not making any rash decisions. I'll keep in mind what you said and try to take it as it comes."

"Good. One day at a time, and remember God knows all about it."

"Right. But I can't help wondering sometimes if I really belong in this uniform. Maybe I don't have what it takes."

"Don't say that. You've saved lives. Every day you're serving your country. Even if you don't stay in for the long haul, you've contributed a great deal." He turned her gently toward him. "And, Caddie, we wouldn't have met if you hadn't enlisted. This wasn't a mistake. It may be a step on the path to something different, but don't ever think it was a mistake."

⁂

When the *Wintergreen* docked on September 6 after a three-week deployment, Caddie could feel autumn in the air. All hands were instructed to bring their cold weather gear on the next cruise.

With ten days in port, she had a reasonable hope of seeing Aven before she sailed again, though his cutter was not at its mooring when she arrived home.

The next day, she was due on deck to help with the refitting of the ship, after which she could enjoy a three-day furlough. Before she left her apartment for the day, she took an unexpected phone call from Oregon.

"Miss Lyle?"

"Yes." She didn't recognize the voice, and anyone connected to her life in the Coast Guard would address her as "Boatswain's Mate Lyle" or "Petty Officer Lyle."

"This is Marshall Herting of the *Oregonian*."

Caddie caught her breath. "Oh, hello."

"I've been looking at your story on Kodiak. I like it very much."

It was a good thing he couldn't see her, with the silly smile she wore. "Thank you very much."

"We'd like to feature it in our next weekend edition. We'll be mailing you a check."

"That's wonderful. Thank you."

"Do you have any more travel stories?"

"Well, I. . .no, not really. I haven't prepared any, that is. I'm sure I could. Do you want more stories on Alaska?"

"We'd rather see some other destinations. Do you live in Alaska?"

"No. Yes. Well, for now." She swallowed hard. "See, I'm in the military."

"Oh?"

"Yes, sir. I'm in the Coast Guard. I'm stationed at Kodiak for now."

"Ah. That explains your choice of subject." After a pause, he said, "You did an excellent job on the story. You must have spent a lot of time preparing it."

"Quite a bit, but I enjoyed it. I was able to talk to several hunting and fishing lodge operators while I was off duty."

"Well, your photos are fantastic. Made me want to run out and buy a ticket to Kodiak."

Caddie laughed. "Come next summer. It's starting to get chilly here now."

"I may do that. Contact me if you come up with any more ideas."

"Thank you, sir. I will."

She clicked off her phone, smiling. The money from the article wasn't a huge amount, but the satisfaction she felt made up for that.

Quickly she keyed in her grandmother's number. "Hi, Gram? It's Caddie. I'm sorry to call so early, but I'm due at work in a few minutes."

"Hello, dear," came her grandmother's warm voice. "What are you up to?"

"I wanted to tell you that your paper is buying my story. They'll run it next weekend."

Gram's crowing could surely be heard throughout her senior citizens' complex. "Sweetie, that's terrific! I knew you could do it! You always used to write cute stories, and those pictures you sent home last spring were amazing. Now, what are you going to do next?"

"Next?" Caddie blinked. Apparently Gram wasn't satisfied with one article. "Well, Mr. Herting did ask if I had any more travel stories in mind. But I can't travel now."

"Hogwash. You travel all the time."

"Well, yeah, but he didn't want a whole series on Alaska."

"Can't you do research on the computer for other places?" Gram asked.

"Well, maybe, but it wouldn't be the same as going to the destination."

"I know. You'll just have to sell Alaska articles to other newspapers. Magazines, too."

"Oh, Gram, I don't know. I don't have enough free time to figure all that out."

"But, sweetie, you're a natural. I've kept that letter you wrote me when you'd been to Homer. It made me cry. And the pictures you took of the mountains and the ship your daddy sailed on and that funny little lighthouse."

Caddie frowned. "You mean the Salty Dog?"

"That's it."

She stifled a laugh. The Salty Dog was a bar frequented by tourists on Homer Spit. Caddie had snapped the photo because of the odd architecture of the historic building-turned-tavern.

"Oh, Gram, I don't know."

"A lot of magazines have travel stories, not just travel magazines. My women's magazines each have one every month."

"Hmm." Caddie recalled a decorating magazine she'd seen in the doctor's office with an article about a New England farmhouse. Maybe they would take an article about decorating with Native Alaskan art. She was sure Jo-Lynn could help her find some local artists and collectors. "I'll think about that when I have time. Thanks, Gram! I love you."

ten

In late September, the *Milroy* plied the waters of Prince William Sound and Cook Inlet, checking salmon, cod, and scallop catches. Aven's sporadic communication with Caddie kept him eager for the next e-mail or phone call.

When his ship put in at Seward for half a day, he tried her cell phone but couldn't get through. Her ship was scheduled to take supplies to scientists doing research in the Walrus Islands State Game Sanctuary in Bristol Bay. But her latest e-mail came through just fine.

> *Hey, I've been thinking a lot about what you and my Gram said about my pictures and writing. That article for the newspaper got my ambition bubbling, and I've gotten guidelines for several magazines by e-mail. I had a chance this morning to get some fantastic shots of walrus in the wild, and now I'm looking for magazines that might be open to a photo essay. There's one that's looking for stories about women in unusual jobs, and I thought immediately of your sister, Robyn. Do you suppose she'd let me photograph her sometime? Gotta go! I miss you.*

Aven smiled as he reread the message. He clicked on "REPLY" and typed:

> *I think that's a great idea, but you realize that to photograph Robyn and her dogs, you'd have to be within a thousand miles of her, right? Not that I think you can't*

*do it. You've got the ingenuity to make it happen. Let's
pray for a chance to go to Wasilla together.*

He hesitated for a moment. Taking Caddie home to
meet the family would be a huge step. He'd never brought
a woman home before. His mother and Robyn—even
Grandpa—would assume things were sailing full steam
toward permanence. Did he want them to think that?

In spite of the slightly scary factor, the idea sat well
with him, and he clicked "SEND." Too late to take back the
invitation. Now for the prayer. It would be next to impossible
to get a long enough leave for both of them at the same time.
But then, God specialized in the impossible.

❧

Caddie ducked into the crowded cabin she shared with
Operations Specialist Lindsey Rockwell. Bunks, lockers, a
shared desk—those took up most of the space. But Caddie
was used to tight quarters on a ship.

She was thankful to have other women aboard, even
though Lindsey seemed a bit standoffish. The other two
females—who bore the rank designation "seaman" despite their
gender—had quarters nearby. Those two talked more than
Lindsey, and in Dee Morrison's case sometimes to the point of
annoyance. Because of the nature of her duties, Caddie didn't
spend much time with Dee or her roommate, Vera Hotchkiss.

Lindsey was stretched on her bunk, the bottom one,
which she'd occupied long before Caddie was transferred to
the *Wintergreen*.

"Hi," Caddie said. "Whatcha reading?" She smiled and
watched Lindsey's face to gauge her mood.

"Just a magazine."

Her listless voice set Caddie's internal mood gauge at
"bored, a little tired, but not hostile." Did Lindsey resent her?
Caddie had been away from the ship for more than a month.

Had Lindsey wished she wouldn't return and reclaim her space in the cabin?

Caddie stooped and caught a glimpse of the cover. "That looks interesting. Do they have travel stories?"

"Travel? I guess so. Why? Are you taking a vacation?"

Caddie laughed. "No. I'm earning extra money by writing travel stories."

"For real?" Lindsey sat up and swung her legs over the edge of the bunk. "Is that what you've been working on with the laptop?"

"Yeah. I'm trying to sell articles and pictures."

"You take good pictures."

"Thanks." Caddie peeled off her jacket and hung it in her locker. "I heard we may go as far as Nome on our next deployment."

Lindsey shrugged. "Maybe."

"It'll be the farthest north I've ever been. I'd kind of like to see Nome."

"There's not much there. And it's kind of late in the season to head toward the Arctic Circle."

Lindsey flopped back on her bunk, and Caddie wondered if keeping the conversation going was worth the effort. A sudden idea jogged her, but she cast it aside. "So, do you know what we're having for supper?" Even to her, it sounded lame.

"No."

The idea wouldn't go away. Caddie took her hairbrush from her locker and snapped on the clip-on light so she could see what she was doing in the mirror inside the locker door.

Lord, is this thought from You, or is it a crazy whim of mine? I don't want to say something just to get Lindsey to talk. It could turn out all wrong, and I'd regret mentioning it.

She waited but felt nothing. Her hair was disheveled

from the wind, and she began coaxing it into place with her brush.

"Did you get some good pictures when you went out to look at the walrus yesterday?" Lindsey asked.

"Yeah, I did. I'm hoping to sell some, but I'm not sure where yet." Caddie inhaled slowly. Her stomach fluttered, but she decided it was now or never. She turned and smiled at her roommate. "You know what I'd really like to photograph?"

Lindsey looked up from her magazine. "What?"

"You."

"You're not serious."

"Yes, I am."

Lindsey lowered the magazine and stared at her. "Why?"

Caddie smiled. *Hooked. Thank You, Lord. Help me to make good on this.* "I've found a magazine that's interested in profiles of women in unusual jobs. I'd love to do an article on you. Take some pictures of you on the bridge, maybe a few on deck. Then, for a change of pace, take some on shore when we get leave. Give the readers an idea of what our life is like. Four of us women, living on a ship with fifty men."

Lindsey's eyes crinkled. "I don't know. You think they'd buy something like that?"

"Yes, I do." Caddie sat down on the stool they used when sitting at the desk. "I thought about asking Dee or Vera, but let's face it, Dee's not very photogenic. Vera might be okay, but I think what you do is much more impressive. Not only do you live in a man's world, you've begun to climb the ladder of rank. I think it'd be a great story, Lindsey. And your eyes. . ."

"What about my eyes?" Lindsey scowled.

"They're gorgeous. I never know whether they're green or blue."

"Me either. It depends on what color the water is that day."

Caddie laughed and pointed a commanding finger at her. "See, that's part of your uniqueness. Any other woman would have said it depended on what color she wore that day."

Lindsey shrugged. "We've always got the ocean at our backs, or at least it seems that way."

"You're right. And that's what I want to get across. It's lonely out here, even though we're packed in like sardines."

The blue-green eyes flickered, and the ghost of a smile trembled on Lindsey's lips.

Caddie thought how seldom she'd seen Lindsey smile, and how pretty she was in that moment. "It'd make your momma proud," she teased.

At last Lindsey let loose with a genuine laugh. "Do you really think you could sell my story?"

"I'm not sure. But we could have fun trying."

❧

"So what do you want. . .thirty days?" Lieutenant Greer asked.

"No, nothing like that," Aven said quickly. "A week, maybe?"

"Well, you've got time coming. But if I give it to you this month, you'll miss a deployment, and it will wind up being more than a week. If we're not in port when you've finished your business, you'll have to wait until we get back." Greer sat on the edge of his desk, studying the work schedule. "I might be able to give you ten days, starting two weeks from today."

"That's fine, but I don't want you to put the paperwork in yet. I need to get my ducks in a row."

"Oh?"

"Yeah, well. . ." Aven felt his face redden. "I need to coordinate with someone else."

The skipper tilted his head toward his shoulder. "What aren't you telling me, Holland?"

"Nothing you need to know, sir."

Greer's eyes narrowed. "You're not violating regulations, are you?"

"No. Absolutely not."

"Good. So what *are* you doing?"

Aven gritted his teeth. No way to get out of this. "She's on another ship." There. He'd said it.

Greer stared at him for a moment then laughed. "Is that all? Why so secretive?"

"I just. . .I didn't want all the men to know. I'd never hear the end of it."

"I see. All right. It'll be our little secret. Let me know when you want to begin your leave."

"Thank you, sir." Aven left the ward room to the sound of Greer's laughter.

He wasn't at all sure that Caddie could get time off, since she'd just finished a medical leave, but if the timing was right, he might be able to whisk her away for a few days during his ten days off duty. If it didn't work out, he'd just have to wait awhile.

He went in search of Mark and found him in the engine room, where the men had a weight bench and a stationary bicycle—the closest they could come to a gym on board. "Mark, I need your opinion on a private matter." It was a signal they'd worked out between cruises, when Jo-Lynn broke the news that she was pregnant. If Mark wanted Aven to find a quiet spot on the ship and pray with him, he asked for Aven's "opinion."

Now the tables were turned, but Mark picked up the signal, grabbed his towel, and followed Aven into the companionway. "What's up?"

"Didn't mean to interrupt your workout."

"It's okay."

Aven looked over his shoulder. So far, so good. A few seconds might be all they got alone. "Would you pray for Caddie and me? I want to take her home to meet my family, but we'd need at least three or four days. That's if we fly.

She'll make a fuss if I try to pay for plane tickets, but I doubt she can take more time off, since she just had all that medical leave."

"Yeah, that could be tough to pull off."

At that moment, the ship's bell rang. Aven checked his watch. "I've got to run. I'm taking a detail to inspect another boat this afternoon."

"Have fun. I'm off until tonight."

Aven hurried up the ladder to the main deck. Just as he came into the open, his radio burbled. "Boatswain's Mate Holland, please report to the bridge."

Seaman Kusiak and another man had come on deck, and Aven called, "I'll be right with you." He hurried up to the bridge.

Greer waited. "The U.S. Marshal's office just informed us that the fishing boat we impounded in June is being auctioned in Anchorage."

"The *Molly K*?"

"That's the one."

Aven wondered why this was important to him. Impounded boats were sold at auction, and the money was put toward law enforcement equipment. The crews who made the arrests and impoundments weren't usually involved in that end of the case. "Is there a problem?"

"They're not sure. Seems Captain Andrews placed a bid on his boat."

"He's allowed to do that."

"Yes." Greer frowned and looked down at the printout in his hand. "But Andrews filed for bankruptcy after we took the boat. Now he shows up with a large chunk of cash to bid on it."

"And they want to know where he got it."

"That's right."

Aven followed his skipper to the big windows that looked out on the sea ahead. His team waited down on the main deck. In the distance, several fishing boats bobbed on the shallow waves.

"Is the marshal's office looking into it?"

"They may hand it to the state police," Greer said. "I told him we didn't have any information about Andrews's income, other than his fishing business, but we'll share anything we turn up."

Aven nodded. "It's unlikely that we will come across anything. Now, we might run into some of his former crew members in other places."

"Yeah." Greer sighed. "Well, I just wanted to let you know and to tell you to watch your back, Holland. You never know when one of those fishermen who attacked you will show up on another boat you're inspecting. And they carry grudges, believe me."

❧

Caddie used her morning free time to photograph Lindsey at work on the bridge. With Captain Raven's permission, she took her camera to Lindsey's communications center while the ship sailed steadily toward civilization, on its way to refit buoys within Cook Inlet. She hoped they would get to go ashore in Anchorage, as she'd never seen the city, and perhaps Homer. She wouldn't have much chance to build her portfolio of wildlife photos, but she'd have breathtaking backdrops for her photos of Lindsey. The inactive volcanoes around Kachemak Bay would be perfect if they did stop at Homer. And while they sailed, with only ocean on every side, she found Lindsey a more accessible subject.

"I feel silly with you hanging around with that camera," Lindsey said with a scowl.

"Just do what you normally do," Caddie told her. "I'll snap a few candid pictures while you're working."

"It's too weird. The guys are all distracted, wondering what we're up to."

Caddie had wondered if the occasional stares the officer of

the deck and two other petty officers at work threw their way would rattle her model, but she'd secured the go-ahead from Captain Raven in advance, and she wasn't going to throw away her chance.

"Ignore me," she said. "Ignore those guys, too."

She found that Lindsey was most relaxed when she stood back several paces and used her zoom lens to get the close-ups she wanted.

When Lindsey's shift was over, they went below to the mess hall and got a cup of coffee.

Sitting in a corner with her notebook on the knee of her blue uniform pants, Caddie smiled at her roommate. "Let's talk a little bit about your background. I don't think you've ever told me why you joined the Coast Guard."

Lindsey hesitated. "You want the truth?"

"Of course." Caddie smiled, but her interviewee wasn't smiling.

"I wanted to get away from home." Lindsey inhaled deeply, not meeting her gaze. "Things weren't good between me and my folks. I wanted out of there as soon as I graduated."

"Wow. That surprises me." Caddie couldn't help the mental contrast between her own years of longing to enlist in the branch of service that her father was a part of and Lindsey's apparently random choice. "Why the Coast Guard, though? Why not the army or the navy?"

Lindsey shrugged. "Their recruiter came to my school first."

Caddie forced herself to look down at her notebook and scribbled a doodle on her paper, pretending to take notes.

When she glanced up, Lindsey's nerves again showed in her sober face, and she twisted her mug back and forth in her hands. "I'm not sure I'd want you to print that in a magazine."

Caddie leaned toward her and lowered her voice. "I'm sorry. I didn't mean to barge right in on a sensitive topic. And

I'd never put something you're uncomfortable about in the article."

Lindsey licked her lips. "Okay. Well, maybe we can talk about something else and come back to that later."

"Sure." Caddie sat back and checked her list of questions. "What do you like best about your job?"

"Hmm. I have to think about that. I suppose knowing I've done a good job. At least in the military, you know when you're doing okay and when you're not."

"How do you mean?"

Lindsey sipped her coffee and paused for a moment, looking off into space. "It's just that before. . .well, at home mostly. . .I never knew if I was going to get yelled at or what. I liked school better, because if I worked hard there and stayed out of trouble, I could do well. For the most part, the teachers were fair. And that's what I found in the Coast Guard. Basic training was tough, but I knew when I passed each part that I'd succeeded."

"You must have done well in your advanced training, too."

"Pretty well, I guess." Lindsey straightened her shoulders. "I was determined to make it. Because I wasn't going back. I had nothing to go back to."

Caddie studied her pinched face. Although sorrow shadowed her heart, Lindsey didn't want pity; she could see that. "You've done a good job."

Lindsey's features relaxed. She closed her eyes for a moment then opened them, still determined but less wary. "Thank you."

"It was different for me. I didn't want to get away from home so much as I wanted to get into the Coast Guard. My father was—"

"I know. Your father was an illustrious officer."

Caddie felt stung. Was this what had caused the underlying animosity she'd felt emanating from Lindsey since she'd transferred to the *Wintergreen*?

"Yes," she said softly. "I wanted to be like him. Now I wonder if my ambition was misdirected."

"Oh? He *was* a good officer. I've heard people talk about him."

"Yes, but. . .I'm not so sure he was a good father." Caddie squirmed a bit in her chair.

Okay, Lord, I'm supposed to be doing the interviewing here. Do You really want me to talk about this?

"Then why did you want to please him so badly?"

"That's just it. I didn't think that was my motive. At least, I never used to look at it that way, but. . .well, a lot of the time, Dad wasn't there. He was always off at sea. Mom stayed home with us kids, and she never got bitter about it. She built him up as a hero for us."

"What's wrong with that?"

"I don't think we ever really knew Dad for the man he was. Only the man we *thought* he was. Because we could only snatch time with him here and there. I'm not saying he wasn't a good person. Only that I didn't really know. And I think that might be why, as a kid, I fixated on joining the service. To be like him. To have that in common with him. To have something special with him that I'd never had before."

Lindsey sighed. "Well, trust me, a dream kind of father is way better than the kind of father I had. At least you didn't have to run away from him."

They sat in silence. A couple of sailors came from the galley and began restocking the supplies for the next meal.

Caddie thought about Lindsey's words. *Dear Lord, I don't think I've ever really appreciated the father You gave me. Please show me how to relate to Lindsey in a way that will help her.*

Her pulse picked up as she wondered what to say. Why was it so hard? Maybe because she'd always figured Lindsey would sneer if she tried to talk to her about spiritual things.

"You know," she said at last, "you're absolutely right. Even though my dad had some faults, and even though he never spent as much time at home as we all would have liked, he wasn't bad as fathers go. And I miss him a lot." Tears welled in her eyes. "These past few years, I've had to rely on my heavenly Father for security."

Lindsey's eyebrows shot up and that "Here it comes" expression crept over her face.

Caddie plunged on. "I've never said much to you about my faith..."

"I've seen your Bible on the desk in the cabin once or twice."

Caddie started to speak but caught herself. Her impulse was to apologize. But should she? She'd tried hard not to make an issue of her faith on the assumption that Lindsey would be offended. Had she instead erred in keeping quiet?

"We never went to church or anything when I was a kid," Lindsey said.

"We always did."

"Is that why you read the Bible? Because you were brought up that way?"

"I suppose it was at first. But now I read it because I want to. It tells me what God expects and how I should live. Best of all, it tells about Jesus Christ, and how He died for my sins."

Lindsey shook her head. "I never understood any of that—how people think that one person somehow took care of all the evil in the world. You only have to look around to see that it's still there. How did Jesus's dying help?"

Caddie inhaled slowly. She tended to sort all that she knew into mental pigeonholes. Which one should she reach into? "Okay, first of all, Jesus didn't die to clean up the world."

"He didn't? I thought everybody's sins were supposed to

be wiped out somehow when He died."

"Well, in a way. . ." Caddie glanced at her watch. "You know, I have to report for duty in about twenty minutes. I'm not trying to get out of this conversation. I really want to discuss it with you. But I need to be where my Bible is when we talk about it. That way I can show you what God says in the Bible about sin and forgiveness."

"I don't know." Lindsey shook her head. "It doesn't make sense to me."

"But you've never read the Bible, have you?"

"No. I saw the Charlton Heston movie."

Caddie smiled. "There's a lot more to it than that. Look, tomorrow morning we're both free. Let's talk then, okay?"

"I guess so. What about the article?"

"Oh, I'm going to finish it. I'll work on it some tonight, and I'll need to ask you some more questions, but this is really important. About God, I mean."

Lindsey nodded slowly. "All right." She stood and reached for Caddie's coffee mug. "Just, please, if I tell you to stop, you won't keep on and on about it, will you?"

"No. I'll quit talking about it if you want me to."

"Great. See you." Lindsey walked away toward the window where they left the dirty dishes.

Caddie let out a breath. *Lord, help me to do better tomorrow. Let me get it right the first time so she doesn't tell me to shut up. Please?*

eleven

Aven stared at the computer screen and scowled. No matter how he worked it out, Caddie couldn't get enough time off to go to Wasilla with him for at least two months. The *Wintergreen* would dock next week while he was at sea, but only for a few days, and then the ship would head out on a six-week cruise. Caddie would have to be back in Kodiak in time to join her ship for that cruise. No excuses.

He had so much leave stacked up that he really should take some anyway. He ran a hand through his hair, unable to decide what to do.

His cell phone rang, and he pulled it out. "Yeah, Holland."

"This is Lieutenant Greer. A gentleman is here from the U.S. Marshal's office, wanting to speak to you."

"Me?" Aven cast about the recesses of his mind for a reason.

"Affirmative."

A few minutes later, Aven boarded the *Milroy* and entered the wardroom.

Greer stood and gestured toward a lean, middle-aged man wearing a suit. "Holland, this is Deputy U.S. Marshal Ralph Eliot."

Aven shook his hand.

"You remember I told you about the *Molly K* being auctioned?" Greer asked as they all sat down.

"Sure," Aven said. "And the former owner bid on her."

"That's right. Have a seat. Eliot, here, has more news about that." Greer nodded to the deputy marshal.

"Jason Andrews bought his boat back," Eliot said. "Paid cash for it. Forty-seven grand."

Aven gave a low whistle. "I thought he filed for bankruptcy. How could he have that much socked away?"

"That's the question." Eliot reached into his inside jacket pocket and took out a small notebook. "This summer, Andrews was practically going bust. You know how all the fishermen have complained that the catch is poor this year."

"Yeah," Aven said. "They have to go farther to fill their quotas."

"Uh-huh. Well, Andrews was falling behind on his house payments. He told his bank in June he couldn't make the regular payment. They cut him some slack and let him refinance. Then he loses the boat. Financial disaster, right? But then he comes up with all this money for the boat on a couple of months' notice."

"He didn't sell the house, did he?" Aven asked.

"Nope. He and his wife are still living in it, along with three daughters and one grandkid."

"Okay, I give up. Where did the money come from?"

"That's what we'd like to know. The scuttlebutt is that the men of his crew scraped it up for him."

Aven pulled back and frowned. "That doesn't make a lot of sense. His men were worse off than he was. How could the six of them come up with that much money?"

"That's a good question. And did they just do it out of the goodness of their hearts?"

Aven thought about it, but it still didn't add up. "Six men pass the hat because they feel bad for their boss and come up with forty-seven thousand dollars in cash? I don't think so."

Greer tapped a pen on his desk. "Maybe some of them had some assets. Or some connections. I wonder if they all felt guilty. After all, from what Holland tells me, it was their fault he lost his boat."

"That's right," Aven said. "I gave Andrews a citation, but then the men started a brawl. That's what clinched it. If they hadn't assaulted us, we never would have impounded the boat."

"That's what I thought." Eliot studied his notebook for a moment then slid it back inside his jacket. "I wanted to check the details of the confrontation with you before I talked to Andrews's crew."

"You're going out and talk to them all?"

"Going to try. Most of them live in the Seward area. That's where Andrews lives. But two of them live out here on Kodiak."

"Spruce Waller being one," Aven said.

Eliot's eyes narrowed. "Yeah. Do you know something about him?"

"Not really. Just that his brother, Clay, has a boat and someone gave us a tip a few weeks ago that he was running drugs." He looked toward Greer. "Our cutter chased him, but he outran us and ducked into a channel we couldn't navigate."

The lieutenant nodded in acknowledgement. "That's right. The tip came in as an anonymous call to our communications center. I learned later that a woman made the call."

Aven continued, "A few days after we tried to run that boat down, I saw Spruce Waller and his brother repainting a boat over at Anton Larsen Bay. I think it was Clay Waller's boat, tied up in front of Spruce's cabin. But I wasn't a hundred percent sure."

"Did you do anything about it?"

"I told the state police, but they didn't seem to give it high priority. They did enlarge the pictures I gave them and confirmed the two men doing the painting were Spruce and Clay Waller."

Greer scratched his jaw. "We speculated that after we impounded the *Molly K*, Spruce Waller may have started working with his brother, but we don't have any hard evidence."

Aven nodded. "So what if the Waller brothers are running drugs, and some of that drug money went to buy Captain Andrews's boat back?"

Eliot drew in a deep breath. "That would be hard to prove."

"But if you *could* prove it, you'd put the drug runners away," Aven said.

"Yes, and we'd get to auction the *Molly K* again." Eliot smiled. "Any ideas on how we might do that?"

Aven's adrenaline surged. Finally, he could *do* something. "I'd be happy to go with you when you interview the two crewmen who live near here."

"Great." Eliot brought out the notebook again. "Spruce Waller and Terry Herman. Both live in Kodiak."

"I'm free this afternoon. Let's try Herman first," Aven suggested. "He may be easier to catch up with than Waller."

Half an hour later, Aven stood back and let Eliot knock on the door of a weathered duplex.

A baby was crying inside. The door swung open, and the wailing increased in pitch.

A young woman gazed at them. "Yes?" Her plain features hovered between curiosity and fear. Aven took in the ragged flannel shirt she wore over a tank top and faded jeans. No makeup. Her only jewelry consisted of a wedding ring and a cheap digital watch.

"I'm Deputy U.S. Marshal Ralph Eliot, and this is Petty Officer Aven Holland with the Coast Guard. We'd like to speak to Terry Herman."

The young woman looked them up and down, eyeing Eliot's suit and Aven's uniform. Aven wondered if he should be watching the back door. The baby's wails became screams.

"Come on in." She swung the door wide open and turned to scoop the baby out of a mesh playpen. "Terry, you got company." She and the baby disappeared through a doorway, and the crying stopped.

A lanky young man in jeans and a faded black T-shirt unfolded himself off the sofa and stood eyeing them. Eliot again made the introductions.

Herman nodded at Aven. "I recognize you. Am I in trouble again? Because I paid my fine."

"We just want to ask you some questions," Aven said.

Herman hesitated then shrugged. "As long as I'm not in trouble." He plopped back down on the sofa and nodded toward a ragged armchair. "Have a seat."

Eliot crossed to the sofa and sat on the end farthest from Herman. Aven took the chair.

"Mr. Herman," Eliot said, "what are you doing for work now?"

Herman huffed out a breath. "Nothing at the moment. I've got a lead on a job. Got to do something when you have a family."

"How have you been living for the last couple of months?"

"Off our savings. It's gone now, though. Crystal's folks helped us some, but I'm probably going to start at the cannery soon." He wouldn't meet Eliot's eyes.

"You're not going to work for Jason Andrews again?" Aven asked.

"Not hardly. He lost the boat."

Eliot said, "You didn't hear? He bought it back at auction a few days ago."

"Huh. No, I didn't know."

"I heard a rumor that his crew had got up the money so Captain Andrews could bid on the boat."

"Maybe so."

"Did you help raise the money?" Eliot asked. "Is that where your savings went?"

Herman rose and walked over to the window. He stood with his hands on his hips, his back to them. "No. I didn't have anything to do with that. We didn't have much put away, and we've spent it mostly on food and rent."

"Do you know who did get the money for Andrews?"

Herman turned and shook his head, staring at Eliot. "Look, I paid my fine. They said if we hadn't gotten into that fight, nobody would have been arrested and the skipper would have kept the boat. Well, it wasn't my fault." He looked over at Aven, his dark eyes anxious. "I'm sorry about what happened. It wasn't my idea to jump you and your men. If it was up to me, we wouldn't have done it. But Spruce was riled, and all the others said they'd back him up. I felt like I had to take part. I got a few licks in, I admit it, but I paid my fine, and I've got a record now. And no, I don't want to go back to working with them again. I want to stay out of jail. Like I said, I've got a kid now. I need to be working a steady job, not mixing it up with the Coast Guard."

Aven caught his gaze and held it for a long moment. "Apology accepted."

Eliot took out his pocket notebook and jotted in it. "Are you saying you think you'd get into trouble again if you went back to work for Captain Andrews?"

"I dunno."

"How long had you worked for him?"

"Just since spring."

"And before that?"

The young man walked back to the sofa and plunked down on it. "I used to go out with Ned Carson's crew. But he died, and his widow sold his boat to someone off the island. So when I heard this Andrews fella needed men last spring,

I jumped at it. Needed a berth on a boat, and I didn't ask questions."

Aven leaned forward and asked, "Who told you about the job?"

"One of the men working on the *Molly K.*"

"Spruce Waller?" Eliot asked.

Herman swiveled and stared at him. "Yeah. How. . ."

Eliot shrugged. "He's the only other one of Andrews's crew who lives in Kodiak. How did he connect with Andrews, do you know?"

"No. I think he'd been with him awhile, though. I was hard up for work, and I heard Spruce at a bar one night, talking about leaving to go salmon fishing, so I asked him if they needed help. He said his boss might be hiring and to go with him the next morning. That was that."

"Okay," Eliot said, scribbling in the notebook. "And what's Spruce doing now?"

"I don't know. Haven't seen him since the hearing." Herman's eyelashes lowered and screened his dark eyes.

"Are you sure?" Aven asked.

The young man jerked his head around to look at him. "He went to jail. I was glad I didn't, except for that one night. Since I heard Spruce was out, I've stayed away from places I thought he might be."

"Bad blood between you and Waller?" Eliot stopped writing and arched his eyebrows.

"Not really. But I don't want there to be. Waller's trouble."

"In what way?"

Herman clamped his lips together and shook his head.

Aven bent toward him and clasped his hands together loosely. "Terry, if you know anything it would be in your best interests to tell us."

"Is that a threat?"

"Not at all. But we're going to talk to every man who was on the *Molly K* the day of the fight. We know Captain Andrews didn't have the money to buy the boat back. But he came up with it, and we *will* find out where he got the cash."

"And if we find out you knew," Eliot growled, "you can kiss your wife and baby goodbye, because you'll be doing time for obstructing justice." He rose and stood over Herman, his notebook dangling from his hand. "If you know anything at all, now's the time to speak."

"Terry, tell them about Spruce." The young woman stood in the doorway behind Eliot. She held the baby up against her shoulder and patted his back as she spoke. "If you don't tell, you could get in worse trouble from them than you will from the Wallers."

❧

"Hey, that's great. Hold it!" Caddie snapped the shutter. "Fantastic." She bounded the few steps to Lindsey and showed her the last few shots on the digital camera's small screen.

Lindsey nodded grudgingly. "Not bad. You're a good photographer."

"Thanks. And that necklace is perfect for you." Caddie smiled through gritted teeth and whispered, "Too bad it's only four hundred dollars."

Lindsey chuckled and took the silver and carved wood necklace off. "Yeah, it's really sweet." She went to the counter and handed the necklace back to the shop owner. "Thank you very much."

"I'll be sure to mention your shop in the article," Caddie said, tucking the woman's business card into her pocket.

As they walked outside into the cool sunshine, Lindsey zipped her jacket. "It would be easy to spend a lot of money in a hurry here."

They ambled down the sidewalk in Homer. Most of the

tourists had left a month ago, and many of the shops had closed for the season.

"I'm glad we got a chance to have some time ashore together," Caddie said. "If we get enough pictures today, I may be able to finish putting the article together while we're docked in Kodiak next week. Maybe I can send it off before we put out for the long cruise."

"That'd be great." Lindsey paused to study a window display of embroidered sweaters.

"Just don't get your hopes too high," Caddie reminded her. "There's no guarantee the magazine will buy it."

Lindsey shrugged. "It's been fun doing it anyway. And I'm glad we got to know each other better."

"Me, too." Caddie smiled at her.

Getting to know Lindsey had turned out to be the best part of this deployment. For the past three days, they had studied the Bible together during their off-duty hours. Caddie had shown her friend several scripture passages about sin, forgiveness, and salvation through faith in Christ. Her curiosity whetted, Lindsey had asked if she could borrow Caddie's compact Bible and started reading through the Gospels on her own.

"Hey, look," Caddie said, nudging her. "Cups Café. Isn't that the one Dee and Vera were going to have lunch at?"

"Yes. It's darling." Lindsey tilted her head back to look at the wildly painted teacups and saucers on the roof of the little building. "We've got to eat here. Let me snap your picture under the sign first."

After she took the photo, they went inside and paused just inside the door to exclaim over the stained glass panels and handcrafted objets d'art throughout the crowded room.

"There they are!" Caddie had spotted Dee and Vera at a table in a far corner, waving frantically. "Let's join them. I don't see any other free tables." She and Lindsey squeezed between the diners and reached the other two young women.

"Imagine, the entire female contingent of the *Wintergreen* here at the same time," Dee said with a laugh. She gestured to the ornately decorated dining room. "Like it?"

"Love it," Caddie said.

"We're about finished," Vera told her, "but you two can have our table."

"Thanks." Lindsey picked up a glass-beaded napkin ring. "I think I want to live here."

"Order the Cobb salad. It's great." Dee slid out of her chair. "We've got to head back now. See you later."

As the lunch traffic in the café thinned, the chatter quieted, and Caddie and Lindsey picked up the conversation they'd begun that morning on the way into town.

"I read the last two chapters of Matthew this morning," Lindsey said. "I couldn't stop reading. It was so. . .powerful."

"The Crucifixion and Resurrection?"

"Yes. I wish I knew as much about the Bible as you do. I can't believe I've lived this long assuming I knew what it was about but never read any of it. When do I get to the part about the Ten Commandments?"

Caddie chuckled. "That's in the Old Testament, way back near the beginning. You're reading about the time when Jesus lived, which was much later than Moses."

"Oh." Lindsey's brow puckered in a frown. "Why did you have me start reading near the end?"

"Because I wanted you to read about Jesus. You had so many questions about why He came to earth and how His death could help us."

"Mmm. I get it. And what I read this morning. . .I mean, if the part we talked about before is true, about Jesus being God, then"—Lindsey's eyes shone with unshed tears—"it makes sense to me now. He *had* to be the one to pay for our sins."

Caddie reached over and squeezed her hand. "Just wait

until you read John. There's so much there about Jesus's nature and His ministry. Oh, I'm going to ask the waitress if there's a bookstore near here. I want to get you a Bible of your own and see if I can find a good, basic study book. That will help answer your questions."

"You're teaching me a lot. I appreciate it."

"Thanks, but I seem to be going at it in a haphazard fashion. I keep wondering if I've skipped over something important. Maybe we should start reading Genesis at the same time. Begin with creation. A chapter each of the Old and New Testaments every day."

Lindsey's laugh burbled out. "I was sure you were a fanatic of the worst kind. Do you know, I avoided being alone with you in our cabin because I was afraid you'd try to preach to me?"

"Really." Caddie swallowed hard. *Thank You, Lord, for helping me not to have that impulse.*

"Yes. But now I can't wait to have an hour free to talk about the Bible with you. It's crazy."

"Not crazy. It's God's doing."

Lindsey nodded, her eyes glinting. "I believe that now, but a week ago I'd have used that statement as proof that you were off your rocker."

The waitress came to take their orders, and for a minute the friends turned their attention to the menus. When they'd made their decisions and learned where to find a bookstore, Lindsey looked across the small table at Caddie. "I never thought I'd say this, but would you ask the blessing, please? And. . .I've decided to call my folks when we get back to Kodiak. Would you please pray for me, that I'll know how to talk to them and what to say?"

"Of course. And when you think of it, maybe you can pray for me. I've started a new correspondence course for the next rating."

"Still figuring to follow in your dad's footsteps?"

"Unless I feel God's leading me otherwise. So I need to keep with the program—you know, keep studying and learning."

"How will you know if God wants you to do something else?"

Caddie pursed her lips. "Well, I know He wants me to stay with the Coast Guard for at least another year and a half, because that's the obligation I have left. But after that. . .who knows? I've decided to keep on as though this is my career for the next fourteen years or so. I want to be ready if it is. And if He has something else for me, He'll show me how to prepare for that."

"Like going to work for a magazine, maybe?"

"I doubt it, but. . .you just never know, do you?" Caddie wondered if Lindsey longed for a family and a real home. The question was on her list for the article, but she hadn't quite had the nerve to ask it yet. Voicing the question would force her to face her own yearnings, and they seemed to be stronger since she'd met Aven.

A woman bustled into the restaurant and joined a young man at a table near Caddie and Lindsey. Her smart black jacket and pants, paired with a lavender silk shirt, pegged her in Caddie's mind as a businesswoman, not a tourist.

"Sorry I'm late," she said to the man.

He jumped up to hold her chair. "You're not late. I got here a few minutes early. I was going to stop at the Hailey Gallery down the street, but they're closed. I thought they were staying open this fall."

"Didn't you hear?" the woman asked. "They've been robbed."

Caddie raised her eyebrows at Lindsey to see if she had overheard. Lindsey pulled a sympathetic face.

"That's awful," the man said. "What happened?"

"It was in the paper. Someone hauled over twenty thousand dollars' worth of scrimshaw and carvings out of there sometime Sunday night."

Lindsey leaned toward Caddie and whispered, "That's fifty of those necklaces I modeled for you."

Caddie nodded. It wouldn't take long for thieves to snatch up a valuable inventory in this neighborhood.

"Hey," said Lindsey, and Caddie snapped back to attention.

"You said something?"

Lindsey grinned. "Yes. Dessert is on me."

❧

Terry Herman's face clouded and he scowled at his wife. "Shut up, Crystal."

Aven wished he were elsewhere.

"No." She stepped forward. "This is what got you arrested in the first place."

"How do you figure?" Terry asked.

"You knew stuff was going on, but you kept quiet. So instead of getting arrested for drugs, you got pinched for assaulting fisheries cops."

"I couldn't rat on guys I worked with."

Crystal scrunched up her face and shook her head. "You could have just quit and tried to get on a better boat. One where they did things legal."

"I told you to shut up."

Eliot held out one hand in supplication. "All right, folks. Let's stay calm." He sent Terry a meaningful look. "Mr. Herman, as I said before, if you have information that could help our investigation, now is the time to speak. Because withholding stuff like that is a crime."

Terry lowered his head into his hands. "Man, oh, man. Why can't you shut up, Crystal?" He looked up at Eliot. "If I talk to you, Spruce Waller and his brother will find out. No telling what they'll do."

"They won't do much if they're in jail," Eliot said.

Aven glanced over at Crystal. "Mrs. Herman, would you have any coffee?"

She stared at him as if he'd asked for champagne, but after a moment her tight features relaxed. "Sure." She crossed the room and laid the baby on a blanket in the playpen. He stirred and whimpered, then lay still. Crystal went into the kitchen, and Aven heard water running.

Eliot arched his eyebrows at Aven, as though inquiring if he wanted to speak.

Aven nodded and said quietly, "Terry, your wife is right. Talking to us is the best thing you can do right now."

"What if I say no? Are you going to arrest me again?"

Eliot sat down again and let out a breath. "Not today. But I can make it difficult for you to find work, and I'd really like to see you working again. You've got a nice family. You should be bringing home a paycheck, not bouncing in and out of the court system."

Terry stared at the threadbare carpet for a long moment, his lips twitching. At last he looked to Aven. "Listen, you gotta believe me. I don't really know anything, just things I heard the other guys say on the boat, you know?"

"Tell us what you heard," Aven said.

"Spruce Waller's not the main one you want. It's his brother, Clay."

"He's running drugs into Alaska on his boat," Aven said.

Terry's eyes widened. "Yeah. I mean, that's what I heard. He goes out to sea and meets a boat coming in."

"Where from?"

"I don't know. Hawaii? Mexico? All I know is they don't want to touch land, so Clay goes to meet them and gets the stuff."

"He pays them in cash and passes the stuff on to street dealers?"

Terry frowned and flicked a glance at Eliot but continued to address Aven. "I really don't know what he does with it. And if I'd known he was mixed up in drugs, I never would have gone with him to try to get a job. But I did go with him, and. . .well, I heard that sometimes he sends things out of Alaska when he picks up the drugs."

Aven studied his face. "What kind of things?"

Terry looked over his shoulder toward the kitchen. "Look, Crystal doesn't know this. I didn't tell her. She's got friends. . .her brother's married to a Native Alaskan, you know what I'm saying?"

"No." Aven glanced at Eliot, but the deputy marshal shook his head. "What *are* you saying, Terry?"

Herman lowered his voice and leaned toward him. "They're sending out Alaskan art. Bootleg art. Trading it for cocaine. That's what I heard. Don't know if it's true. But I did see Spruce grab a piece of plastic tape off a buoy one time. Another guy—Rowe, I think it was—said it was a signal that someone on the mainland had some stuff for him."

"What kind of stuff?" Aven asked.

Terry shrugged. "Stuff to trade, I guess. Spruce would tell his brother, and they'd go get it. Captain Andrews found out, and he told Spruce that if he didn't get his boat back for him he'd turn in his brother." He jumped up and walked to the kitchen doorway. "That coffee ready, Crystal?"

Eliot said softly, "There've been several big heists on the Kenai Peninsula. Some high-end art galleries and shops have been hit." He started to rise.

"We have to drink the coffee," Aven hissed.

"Okay, but the quicker the better."

Crystal came into the room carrying two steaming mugs. Terry followed with a plastic half-gallon milk jug and a sugar bowl with a spoon sticking out of it.

"Just milk," Aven said. He accepted a mug from Crystal

and poured as much milk into it as he could to cool it down.

Crystal walked over to Eliot and handed him the other mug. "Did he tell you?"

"He's been very cooperative," Eliot said. "We'll try not to let anyone know, though."

"Good." She went to the playpen and leaned over it for a moment, watching the baby. She straightened, glanced at her husband, and walked out of the room.

"Look, that's it," Terry said. "I really don't know anything solid. It's just rumors."

"That's right," Aven said with a smile.

"And you didn't tell us anything," Eliot added.

Aven gulped down half his coffee and held the mug out. "Thanks. Keep your head down. Hey, I think my CO knows someone at the cannery. I'll ask him if he can put in a word for you."

He and Eliot hurried out to the deputy marshal's rental car.

"Waller's house first?" Eliot asked.

"Yes." Aven gave him directions to the apartment building. They arrived a few minutes later, but no one answered the door at Spruce Waller's place.

"Now what?"

Aven said, "Last time I went looking for him, he was at his cabin at Anton Larsen Bay."

"How far is it?"

"You can drive it in twenty or thirty minutes."

Eliot checked his watch. "You up for it? It's almost four o'clock."

"Let's do it."

Aven navigated Eliot over the same roads he'd taken Caddie on earlier. His thoughts flew to the *Wintergreen*, and he prayed for her as they passed the riverside where they'd watched the bears. Another thought occurred to him as he recalled the tip his commanding officer had received about the boat they'd pursued. "You know what?"

"What?" Eliot asked.

"Greer said it was a woman who called in reporting that the boat—which we now know was Clay Waller's—was picking up a drug shipment. It wouldn't surprise me if the one who made that call was Crystal."

At Waller's cabin, they drove into the yard and got out, looking around. Aven looked first for Clay's cabin cruiser, but the slip in the cove was empty. A small aluminum boat lay upside down on shore a few yards from the dock. Spruce Waller's SUV was parked beside the cabin.

As Eliot approached the door, Aven slipped around the side of the building. A back door opened into a lean-to woodshed. Eliot knocked on the front door, but the sound reverberated through the cabin with no response.

After fifteen seconds, Eliot pounded on the door again. Nothing.

Aven stepped into the woodshed and lifted the latch on the back door. It swung wide, and a musty smell of dust and old ashes greeted him. He drew his sidearm. "Eliot?"

"Yeah?"

"I'm going in the back."

Eliot yelled something, but Aven didn't hear it. He was already inside, peering past the muzzle of his pistol into the dim interior of the cabin. He looked all around the back room, which seemed to be Waller's bedroom, then walked through the larger front room. He opened the front door.

Eliot stood on the step outside, a pistol in his hand.

"He's not here," Aven said.

Eliot exhaled and pushed his hair back. "Don't do that again. He could have blown your head off."

"He didn't."

"Yeah, well, there's also the little technicality about search warrants."

Aven blinked as he considered that. "Yeah, true."

Eliot peered past him, looking beyond Aven into the dim interior. "You sure he's not hiding someplace?"

"Pretty sure." Aven turned back into the cabin.

Eliot hesitated, looked over his shoulder, and followed. He did a more thorough search than Aven had with no more results.

"So now what do we do?"

Eliot threw him a resigned glance. "Lock the front door and leave."

"He could be anywhere out here."

"Yes, and he could be watching right now through the scope of a rifle."

Aven squeezed his mouth shut tight and waited for further instructions.

"On the other hand," Eliot said, "he could be out in the boat with his brother. Come on. We might as well go back to Kodiak and have dinner."

They got into the car, and Eliot drove in silence. Several times, Aven started to speak, but thought better of it. He'd definitely broken some rules. Had he come down a notch in Eliot's opinion?

As they neared the shopping district in Kodiak, Aven's phone rang. "Hello."

"Mr. Holland? That is. . .Aven Holland?"

"Yes?"

"This is Brett Sellers. I don't know if you remember me, but I made the dog harness for your sister."

"Of course I remember you."

Eliot looked over with raised eyebrows.

Aven shrugged in apology.

"Yeah, well, I hope she likes it," Sellers said.

"She does. She's very happy with it." Was this going to be a sales pitch for more equipment?

Eliot parked in front of a seafood restaurant, and Aven reached to unbuckle his seatbelt.

"Well, I saw something that could be related to a crime. I didn't want to call the police, but it's been bothering me all day. Then I remembered you and how you have some sort of law enforcement job. I thought maybe I could run it by you, and you could decide whether the police ought to know."

Aven hesitated with his hand on the door latch. "Okay. What is it?"

"There's a shop next to mine that sells souvenirs. You know, plastic totem poles. Plush polar bears."

"Yeah, okay. What about it?"

"I stopped in there this morning before opening time to see if I could borrow a coffee filter. The owner was packing up some merchandise, but it was way better quality than what he usually carries."

Aven frowned. "So? Maybe he's upgrading his inventory."

"No, listen. He wasn't unpacking it. He was wrapping it and putting it in crates. I saw carved walrus tusks and whale baleen."

Aven's heart skipped. "Is the owner a Native Alaskan?"

"No way. His hair's blonder than mine. He claims he has Russian blood, but I'm skeptical."

"Okay. It's possible he bought the things legally. Tell you what." Aven shot Eliot a glance. The deputy marshal was watching him keenly. "There's a man from the U.S. Marshal's office in Anchorage here in Kodiak right now. Can I bring him to your shop in about twenty minutes?"

"Uh, well. . .it might be better if you just went straight to his. I wouldn't want him to know I ratted on him." Sellers sighed. "He'll know anyway, I suppose."

"It could be perfectly innocent," Aven said.

"Could be. Doubt it. He tried to cover it all up quick

when I walked in."

Aven took the name of the souvenir shop and signed off.

Eliot leaned against his car door, waiting. "Well? What was that?" he asked.

"Maybe a wild goose chase. Head down the street. We've got a tip on allegedly stolen artwork."

twelve

When the *Wintergreen* docked in Kodiak three days later, Caddie went straight to her apartment. She would have only one day off before she was expected back on duty to help ready the ship for their long deployment. The wind held the bite of autumn, and the bitter winter of Alaska would come hard on its heels.

Her dreams of a relationship with Aven seemed to slip away with the summer. Would they ever seize enough time together to get to know each other better? Even though his ship was in port, he might not be able to see her. His last e-mail had told how busy he'd been helping the U.S. Marshal's office track down some smugglers.

She didn't even know how long Aven would be posted in Kodiak. What if he were transferred away? Although his family lived in Alaska, he might be transferred thousands of miles away. She would have to ask him about that.

She dropped her sea bag on the rug and wearily sorted the mail she'd picked up. Her spirits lifted when she opened an envelope from the *Oregonian*. The check for her travel story was a nice bonus and would cover most of the Christmas gifts she wanted to buy this year. Already she'd looked over mukluks for Mira and snowshoes for Jordan.

When she came out of the shower half an hour later, the phone was ringing. She ran to answer it, hoping Aven might be on the other end of the connection.

"Hey, you're back!" Jo-Lynn's cheery voice floated to her.

"Yes. How are you doing?"

"Fine, after eleven every morning. Not so good before

139

that. I'm eating like a horse once the morning sickness passes, though. I've got to be careful. Want to come for supper tonight?"

"I think I'd better stay in and get to bed early. How about if I come see you tomorrow?"

"Sure," Jo-Lynn said.

"So. . .I guess Mark's home, too. I saw the *Milroy* at the docks."

"Yeah, they've got a few more days."

I will not ask about Aven, Caddie resolved.

Jo-Lynn saved her the trouble. "Hey, Aven's been tearing into this smuggling case. Did he tell you about it?"

"Not much. Just that he's been busy. I've hardly heard from him in the last week."

"You'll have to get the details from him, but it has something to do with an art theft."

Caddie caught her breath. "When I was in Homer a few days ago, people were talking about an art gallery being robbed. That probably has nothing to do with what you're talking about, though."

"I don't know," Jo-Lynn said. "But I gather there have been a lot of these thefts, and the stolen artwork is being smuggled out of Alaska and sold in Japan and. . .well, like I said, I'm not up on the details, but Mark and Aven were talking about it yesterday."

Caddie slept late the next morning and awoke grumpy and discouraged. Would her relationship with Aven go anywhere or not? She sat on the bed in her flannel pajamas and opened her Bible. Her schedule of reading took her to the last chapter of I Timothy. "But godliness with contentment is great gain," she read. The simple words convicted her.

She had so much—a good job, a loving family, godly friends in Jo-Lynn and Mark, and a new friend in Lindsey.

She was thankful for all of them, she realized, and for Aven, too. But was she content?

Lord, thank You for all You've given me, she prayed. *If Aven and I never move beyond friendship, he is still a wonderful gift from You. Help me to treasure each moment we've had together without demanding more. If You want us to grow closer, I'll cherish the time You give us. If not, then help me not to poison my heart with discontent.*

She rose and dressed in jeans and a wool sweater. If Jo-Lynn didn't feel like going out, maybe Caddie could run some errands for her. She stuffed her cell phone into a deep pocket and grabbed her wallet.

Walking down the street toward the Phifers' duplex, she found that her land legs were wobbly. She'd grown so accustomed to the rolling deck that the pavement seemed unpredictably stagnant.

She found Jo-Lynn eager to get out of the house.

"Mark's got to work all day on the ship. I don't suppose you'd drive me to the grocery store?"

"I'd love to," Caddie replied, snatching the car keys from Jo-Lynn's hand. "My cupboards are bare, and I'm craving fresh fruit."

Jo-Lynn laughed as she reached for her windbreaker. "Hey, I'm the one who's supposed to have cravings."

They spent the day together, and Caddie declined another dinner invitation.

Back in her apartment, she faced an evening alone, determined to continue giving thanks to God. She settled down at the table with her laptop to work on the final draft of her magazine article about Lindsey's career. After a half-hour's work, she phoned Lindsey to check one last detail.

"Hey," Lindsey said. "Remember I told you that I was going to call home this week?"

"Yes. Did you?"

"Uh-huh."

"How did it go?" Caddie asked.

"Well. . .sort of up and down. You know, I hadn't spoken to my parents for more than three years. Mom told me today that. . .that my dad left her. He's been gone over a year."

"Lindsey, I'm sorry."

"Yeah. Well, Mom seemed. . .not happy about it, but almost relieved. It was so weird. I was speechless. And you know what? She wants me to come home at Christmas."

"Are you going?"

"I don't know yet," Lindsey said. "But we talked for quite a while. I think we'll keep on talking. And maybe. . . Well, we'll see. Keep praying for me, okay?"

"Absolutely."

Caddie got the information she needed for the article and went back to work, thanking God for Lindsey's breakthrough with her mother. A knock on the door at eight thirty startled her. She rose and walked toward it, her heart racing. No one called this late.

"Caddie?"

Relief flooded her as she hastened to throw the dead bolt.

"Aven! I'd about decided I wouldn't see you this trip."

"I'm sorry. My original plan was to spend every possible second with you when your ship docked. God had other plans."

They stood eyeing each other awkwardly for a long moment. Caddie at last stepped aside. "Would you like to come in for a few minutes?"

"If you don't mind. I've missed you, and I'd like to tell you what I've been up to."

"I'd like to hear it. Excuse me a minute, and I'll put some coffee on. . .or would you rather have hot chocolate?"

"Chocolate sounds great." Aven's fatigue showed in a

shopworn smile. "Seems like I've been running all week and haven't had time to relax."

"Jo-Lynn and Mark said you've been busy."

He followed her into the tiny kitchen and leaned against the counter while she filled two mugs with water and heated them in the microwave.

"I don't know how much you've heard, but a fellow from the U.S. Marshal's office has been here on the island for several days. He came looking for Spruce Waller and Terry Herman."

"Who's Terry Herman?"

Aven rubbed the muscles on the back of his neck. "That's right, you didn't know about him. Let's see, where should I start? Terry is one of the fishermen from the *Molly K.*"

"The boat you impounded back in June?"

"That's right. See, the *Molly K* was auctioned by the marshal's office a week or two ago."

"Standard procedure." Caddie opened a cupboard and took out the bag of marshmallows she'd bought that morning. Her hands shook slightly as she ripped it open. Mentally she berated herself. After telling herself for days that a permanent relationship with Aven, or the lack of one, would not shake her new serenity, she was trembling at his nearness.

"Yes, but the odd thing about the auction was Captain Andrews, the former owner, not only showed up for the sale... he bought the boat back."

Aven apparently didn't notice her jitters, for which Caddie was thankful. "Good for him."

"Well, yes, I suppose so. Except the marshal's office wants to know where he got the money. Forty-seven thousand in cash."

"Cash?" That sounded odd, she had to admit.

"Yes, and they'd heard that the crew raised the money."

"And this is bad?" She handed him his mug and a spoon.

"Well, yes. Because none of these guys has that kind of money. Or if they do, they shouldn't. So when the deputy marshal—Ralph Eliot, his name is—came out here to talk to the crew who live in Kodiak, I went with him. The first man, Terry Herman, told us he had no proof, but he understood while he worked on the boat that Spruce Waller's brother was running drugs in his boat."

"Just like we thought." Caddie smiled. "Now I'm getting the picture. That's why you've been tied up the last few days. You've been out chasing the Waller brothers again."

"That's right."

She led him into the living room and sat down on the sofa.

Aven sat in the chair across from her.

"So, did you catch them?"

Aven's face drooped. "No. We went to Spruce's apartment and his cabin. He wasn't around. We asked his friends and neighbors, but nobody could tell us where he was. Or if they knew, they wouldn't admit it. We took a small boat— borrowed one of the rescue boats—and went all the way to Larsen Bay to look up Clay Waller. And guess what?"

"He wasn't home either."

"Bingo. His wife said he was away. Again. Said he and his brother went out to scout some boats. They're thinking of buying a fishing boat together, she said. But she had no idea where they went to look at these hypothetical boats."

"Where do you think he is?"

"I don't know, but if I were a betting man, I'd put my money on him and Spruce being somewhere together."

Caddie sipped her cocoa. "They took Clay's boat?"

"Uh-huh."

"Jo-Lynn said something about stolen Alaskan art."

Aven nodded. "Yeah. Terry Herman mentioned it.

He'd heard a rumor that Clay Waller was somehow getting scrimshaw and other artworks on the black market and trading for cocaine. And we actually arrested a man—that is, Ralph Eliot did—who had some stolen artworks in his possession."

Caddie listened avidly as Aven related to her how he'd gone with the deputy marshal to the souvenir shop. "The shop owner, Thomas Harper, refused to admit the stuff was stolen. But Eliot contacted the state police, and the goods Harper was packing to ship matched a list of things stolen from a shop that had just closed for the season."

Caddie inhaled sharply. "Not in Homer?"

"No, here in Kodiak."

"Oh. Well, a store in Homer was robbed just before we docked there last week. Or maybe it was an art gallery."

"That doesn't surprise me. This ring has apparently been hitting businesses in several towns. Most of them, as it happens, are near where men who worked on the *Molly K* live."

"Do you think the whole crew is involved in this art and drug smuggling ring?"

"Not the whole crew. Terry Herman wasn't, and he didn't want to be. He was on the fringe of it and heard bits and pieces. He wasn't going to tell us, but his wife bullied him into it. And I really don't think Jason Andrews was involved. He had some violations of fishing regs, but his business seemed legitimate, and he was out there working hard at catching salmon. I don't think he used the *Molly K* for smuggling. It's Clay Waller who seems to be in the thick of it. And I think he's gotten Spruce and some of his friends to do some work for him."

"You mean. . .drug dealing?"

"I don't think so. But possibly some of the thefts. Since we impounded Andrews's boat and they lost their jobs, some of them are hard up. Clay may have promised them some quick money. If he had a potential buyer for high quality art, he needed to come up with a good supply in a hurry."

"How will the state be able to get enough hard evidence to prosecute them?" she asked.

"They're going to lean on Captain Andrews and see if they can get any more information out of him. We suspect now that he knew what the Wallers were up to and held it over Spruce's head. He definitely has a grudge against Spruce for causing the trouble that lost him his boat."

"So, if he threatened to turn Spruce in unless he gave him the money for the auction. . ."

"That's my take." Aven shrugged. "But Andrews is smart. I doubt he'll spill it. He knows he'll lose the boat again permanently if he does and maybe go to prison, too. If you ask me, the police will have to crack this case through the art theft angle. If they can catch the people stealing art and get them to give up their contacts, the whole ring may fall apart."

Caddie lifted her mug and took another sip. "I guess the police have a better chance than we do of catching the boat owners bringing in drugs."

His thoughtful brown eyes held her gaze. "Caddie?"

"Hmm?"

"I've missed you."

She smiled. "I've missed you, too, and I admit I was wondering if I'd ever see you again."

He raised his chin just a hair. "Mind if I come over there and sit with you?"

"Not a bit."

He brought his mug of chocolate with him but slid his free arm around her as he sat down. "This is more like it. I wish I could say I'd never go away again, but I can't do that."

"I know. I can't, either."

He nodded. "Just so's you know, if I don't come see you

for a while, it's not because I don't want to."

She set her mug on the coffee table and snuggled into the warmth of his embrace.

❧

The *Wintergreen* plunged over the sea amid freezing rain and howling wind. Though it was only mid-October, Caddie was chilled to the bone. She tugged at the hood of her parka and pulled it in tight around her face. The cruel face of the Gulf of Alaska sneered at her today. With the seas so choppy, it would be next to impossible to inspect the buoys they'd set out to examine.

Over the loudspeaker came Boatswain Tilley's grating voice. "All hands stand by for rescue duty. Repeat. . ."

Caddie's radio burbled, and she nestled it close to her ear inside her hood. "Lyle speaking. Over."

"We've spotted a small boat that appears to be in distress at oh-two-five degrees. Prepare your crew to man a workboat."

"Affirmative." She hurried across the deck to Jackson, knowing he wouldn't hear her over the wind unless she got within a yard of him. "Let's get ready to lower the workboat."

As the *Wintergreen* approached the scene, she tried not to think about her last rescue mission in a small boat. All on the buoy deck could see that a thirty-foot motorboat had been thrown up on a rocky island that was mostly underwater at high tide. Buoys they were scheduled to refit clearly marked the safe channel between this treacherous shoal and the mainland, and one on the shore shone brightly. Despite the warnings, the boat had apparently wrecked in the unusually rough seas.

Since the *Wintergreen* was far too large to get close to the damaged vessel, the smaller workboat was pressed into service.

Tilley strode onto the buoy deck as Caddie and several

sailors prepared to launch it. "You stay here, Lyle," he shouted at her. "I'll handle this operation myself."

She opened her mouth and closed it again, but unvoiced questions teemed inside her. Did he think she couldn't handle the boat in this rough water? Was it because she'd been injured last summer in the last major rescue operation she'd conducted? Or was he just spoiling for some action?

She oversaw the launching of the boat with Tilley and three others in it. As soon as they were well under way, she hurried under cover, out of the driving rain and up to the bridge.

Captain Raven was Officer of the Deck, and he greeted her with a nod.

Using high-powered binoculars, Caddie could clearly see the beleaguered cabin cruiser. The stern rose and fell with the waves, while the bow appeared to be driven up on the rocks. The craft was not about to float loose unless an unusually large wave lifted it, since the tide had begun its gradual receding.

Two men clambered on the rocks near the bow of the boat, apparently inspecting the damage to the hull, while a third stayed in it, waving and shouting to them.

"What will we do?" Caddie asked the captain. "Tow them in?"

"I think the boat's too badly damaged for that. Looks to me like a big hole in the bow. Can't be sure, but it doesn't look seaworthy from here." He squinted again into his binoculars. "We'll be out of daylight in an hour. We'll probably help them secure their boat and then take the men off the island. They can go back when the sea is calmer and salvage their boat."

Caddie stood beside him as they watched the *Wintergreen*'s workboat approach the rocky islet through the turbulent waves. When Tilley's boat was within hailing range, she saw the boat stand to. The coastguardsmen were visible on deck, all wearing foul-weather gear. The men on the island waved to them.

"What on earth?" Raven lowered his binoculars for an instant and then looked back through the instrument.

Lindsey was at the radio desk when Tilley's voice came over the staticky airwaves. "*Wintergreen,* this is *Wintergreen 1.* Vessel in distress is declining assistance. Request orders from the OOD."

Raven strode to Lindsey's side and spoke into the radio. "It's too dangerous to leave them out there in this weather. Take them off the island."

"Sir, they've indicated they don't want our help. Request permission to return to the ship. Over."

"Negative. Get those fools out of there."

Lindsey flashed a glance at Caddie, cringing slightly as though she was glad she didn't have to take the orders Raven was giving. If civilians declined assistance, the Coast Guard generally left them to their own devices—unless lives were in danger. Captain Raven must believe the men on the little heap of rock would likely not survive the long night there.

With the frigid rain and buffeting winds, Caddie had to agree. When the tide turned and rose again, that boat, staved up as it was, might float off and sink. Then what would happen to the men? They might be swept off the rocks if the wind and high seas didn't abate.

Captain Raven issued curt orders to the other men on the bridge to keep the buoy tender as steady as possible in its location. To Tilley he relayed a request for the registration number of the stranded boat.

Their momentum and the current had brought the buoy tender closer to the wreck. As the captain gave instructions to move it back, Caddie again studied the island with the aid of binoculars.

She caught her breath. The damaged vessel had the same lines and colors as the one she and Aven had seen the Waller brothers working on at Anton Larsen Bay. Not only that, one of the men on shore had the same hulking shape as Spruce Waller. "Sir?"

"Yes, Lyle?"

"That boat, sir. The one on the rocks."

"What about it?"

"I. . .think I've seen it before, sir."

thirteen

"I can't be sure from this distance," Caddie said, staring through her binoculars at the boat on the rocks. "But when we get the number. . ."

"Where did you see it before?" Captain Raven asked.

"Moored in Anton Larsen Bay, getting a paint job." Quickly she told him about her expedition with Aven and the deputy U.S. marshal's quest for the Waller brothers.

Raven's eyes narrowed. To Lindsey, he snapped, "Get the registration number from Bo'sun Tilley *now*."

He resumed his vigil with his binoculars until Lindsey called to him a few minutes later. "Captain, the name on the hull is *Miss Faye IX*, and the registration number is not currently assigned to any registered boat."

"Check it against the boat registered to Clay Waller of Larsen Bay."

A few moments later, Lindsey said, "Only one digit is different, sir."

"I should have sent more men on this detail." Raven turned to Caddie. "If you were closer, could you swear it was the same boat?"

"I think so, sir."

"And the same men?"

She gulped. "Maybe. I only saw them from a distance and in pictures." Her concern lightened as she realized she had the deciding evidence in her possession. "Sir, I have the photos on my camera's digital card in my cabin."

"Get it."

Five minutes later, she puffed back up the final ladder to

the bridge. Captain Raven was again consulting with Tilley via radio as rain sheeted off the windows.

Caddie approached him with the digital card, and he waved her toward the communications desk. She held it out to her friend, and Lindsey took the little square card and popped it into a slot on the computer console.

"We can't let him see the ones you took of me." The tension in Lindsey's voice prompted Caddie to swing around so that her body blocked Raven's view of the computer screen until Lindsey had located and enlarged the best photo of Spruce Waller standing beside his brother's boat with a paintbrush in his hand.

She turned to Raven. "This is the man I told you about, Captain. He's Spruce Waller, the one who started the fight on the *Molly K* last June that led to the boat's being impounded. This other man, I'm told, is his brother, Clay." She pointed to the second man in the photo.

"He's the one who owns that boat out there?"

"Yes, sir. If it's truly the same boat. There's a better picture of the boat they were working on that day." She asked Lindsey, "Could you please bring up the picture before this one? I didn't zoom in quite so much, and the lines of the boat are clearer. You can also see where they've primed over the boat's name."

Raven studied several of Caddie's digital photos then straightened and went back to the window, staring out and scowling.

"Sir, Boatswain Tilley is calling in again," Lindsey said.

The captain again went to her desk.

"I've told the crew of the craft in distress to prepare for boarding," Tilley said. "They're still objecting."

"Approach with caution," Raven replied. "We believe some of those aboard could be dangerous."

"Captain, there looks to be only three of them."

"Watch yourself, Bo'sun."

"Affirmative."

Tilley's workboat now hovered only yards from the beached cabin cruiser, bobbing on the waves.

"Will they be able to land and remove the crew?" one of the petty officers asked the captain.

Raven rubbed his forehead and gritted his teeth. "That remains to be seen."

The fading light obscured the details of Tilley's maneuvers, but a few minutes later a seaman called in.

"*Wintergreen,* this is *Wintergreen 1.* Request additional personnel and equipment."

Raven's gaze bored into Caddie's. "Lyle, I'm calling for a law enforcement cutter, but we can't wait for them to get here. Take six men in the Zodiac. We'll issue sidearms."

"Aye, aye, sir."

As she dashed for the hatch, she heard him say into the radio, "*Wintergreen 1,* we have *Wintergreen 2* en route to assist you. ETA fifteen minutes. What is your current status?"

～

Aven relayed to Mark Phifer and five other men the orders Lieutenant Greer had given him. "We'll get in close and get an assessment. Be prepared to launch our boat fast, depending on the situation."

The men all agreed.

"Greer will sweep the island with the ship's guns if needed, but we want to avoid casualties if at all possible. Unfortunately, the *Wintergreen* landed some men and got into a confrontation. Shots have been fired, and they couldn't get their men off the island. Our priority is to get those men off safely. If we can catch the Waller brothers, too, that's gravy." He didn't know which personnel were involved in the melee. He hoped Caddie was safe on her ship. Too bad it was raining and nearly full dark now. The conditions would make their mission more dangerous.

As they quickly worked to make sure their small surf boat was ready for their operation, a seaman ran onto the deck. "The skipper sent me down to tell you, so he doesn't have to say it on the radio, in case the smugglers can hear."

"What?" Aven stopped checking their equipment and peered at him. Rain ran off his hood onto the deck.

"The *Wintergreen* sent out a second boat. They have two landing parties ashore now. . .or will have soon. The captain felt those ashore needed relief immediately, so he didn't wait for us. Greer says use extreme caution. We don't want any friendly fire casualties."

Aven set his jaw and looked ahead, where he could make out distant lights in the storm. "Tell the skipper we're ready to launch anytime."

The seaman ran toward the hatch.

Mark clapped him on the shoulder. "Quit worrying, Aven."

"They should have stood off and waited for us."

"Like he said, they thought it was necessary to go in."

Aven sighed, wishing the *Milroy* could go faster. He put his radio close to his ear. He heard what he had dreaded to hear—Caddie's voice from the smaller boat that had deployed from her ship. "This is the *Wintergreen 2*. . ."

❧

The Zodiac, with Caddie and six other crewmen in it, rushed toward the island and Tilley's boat in the twilight. Tilley would have left at least one man on his boat, she knew. The rain still poured down in torrents, and the wind whipped up the waves. Caddie hoped they were not too late to prevent violence. She recalled Aven's account of his past confrontation with Spruce Waller. Even though the burly fisherman knew backup was only minutes away last June, he'd attacked Aven and his men.

Where was Aven now? No doubt hundreds of miles away. She hoped his ship was docked somewhere in a safe haven for the night.

She kept their course as steady as possible, headed for the *Wintergreen 1*. As they approached, she heard Tilley radio the ship. He reported to the captain that his landing party had been fired on and were pinned down on the rocks. Captain Raven instructed the seaman in the workboat to stand offshore further and told Tilley to keep his head down and wait for assistance.

Caddie didn't enter the radio chatter, not wanting to clutter the airwaves. She assumed the smugglers on the island could hear them. Raven's orders to the seaman on the workboat meant he would back off to avoid drawing fire. If the smugglers had thought of hijacking Tilley's boat, that would stymie them.

She instructed Gavin, who was at the helm of the Zodiac, to bring them in on the side of the workboat away from the shore. The seaman on the *Wintergreen 1* and two of the men in the Zodiac secured the smaller inflatable to the workboat so they could talk without using the radio.

"I'm going to land around the other side if I can," Caddie told the seaman she recognized as Michaels. "Can you stand off a little farther so that you're behind us and turn on your spotlights when we're in position? Illuminate them for us. Shine those spots right in their eyes if you can."

"I'll do my best," Michaels said. "But make sure you leave a guard with your boat. They shot at us when we arrived and took out a big window. Tilley told me to back off. I think they've got a shotgun. They might try to rush the Zodiac and get away in it."

"That would be a foolish thing for them to do, but you're right," Caddie said. Desperate men took foolhardy action.

With the smaller Zodiac, Caddie and her party had the

advantage of being able to land directly on the rocky island. She directed Gavin to take the craft around the islet to the side away from the damaged boat. Without running lights, they risked hitting an obstacle, but she felt it was critical to preserve as much surprise as possible. At the spot that appeared to have easiest access for a landing, Gavin nosed the Zodiac to shore.

In minutes, Caddie and five of her six seamen were ashore and climbing over the rocks toward the beached cabin cruiser. After some hesitation, she'd left Dee Morrison with the Zodiac and given her instructions to stand offshore until summoned in.

The islet was little more than a large pile of rocks in the bay, less than a hundred feet long at this stage of the tides, with a blinking buoy on the highest point. At high tide, it would appear to rest in the water. The jagged black rocks in the center hid the damaged boat from Caddie's view, but she could see the stern lights of the *Wintergreen*'s workboat clearly.

She sent one of the young seamen, McQuillan, scrambling to the top of the rocks ahead of her. He jumped back down beside her, panting. "They're holding the bo'sun and his men down behind the rocks on the left. Two-eight-oh degrees. I saw the bo'sun and at least one of his men. There are two of the civilians near their boat's bow and one on board."

Her heart thudded. "Did they see you?"

"I think so."

Caddie nodded and prayed silently for wisdom and safety. The renegades already knew she and her crew were coming.

"What now?" Seaman Torres asked.

"They may not realize how many of us there are," Caddie said. "Three of the *Wintergreen 1*'s crew are ashore. So far as we know, there are three hostile civilians. They may all have small arms."

"Okay," Torres said. "How are we going to do this?"

She crouched behind the boulders and motioned all the men in close. The rain still beat down on them, but the gale had declined to a stiff breeze. "I'm pretty sure these civilians are part of a smuggling ring. For some reason, they're determined not to let us approach them or their boat, even though its hull is caved in. McQuillan says one of them is still on their boat. He's probably monitoring our tactics on the boat's radio. We can't exactly ask Captain Raven or Bo'sun Tilley for instructions or they'd hear our plans."

They all nodded in understanding.

"We six are all armed," she continued. "I expect Tilley is the only one in his landing party with a gun." Standard procedure was for the petty officer to carry a sidearm, but the seamen would not be armed unless danger was anticipated. "We have to assume all three smugglers are armed, though."

"Right," said Torres.

Caddie pulled in a deep breath. "It's pretty dark now. I asked Seaman Michaels on the *Wintergreen 1* to shine his spotlights on the enemy's position on my signal. He's trying to hold his position behind Tilley and his men. If we rush out of the dark, we have a pretty good chance of overrunning the enemy position or at least of relieving Tilley and his men."

"Tilley will help as soon as we make our move," McQuillan said.

"Yes, if he still has ammo."

The men nodded soberly and checked their weapons.

"I'll give them one more chance to give it up," Caddie said. She pressed the call button on her radio.

"This is *Wintergreen 2* landing party. Request *Wintergreen 1* order hostiles to surrender, and if declined, go with our plan. Over."

"Affirmative," said Captain Raven. "Michaels, proceed."

Seconds later, the seaman's voice boomed out over the loudspeaker from the workboat, shouting down the wind. "This is the U.S. Coast Guard. Lay down your weapons and raise your hands over your head."

Caddie and her men inched up the rocks and peered down at the other side of the island.

"Repeat. Lay down your weapons and prepare to be approached by Coast Guard personnel."

A shot rang out from near the beached boat. A man popped up from behind the rocks that covered Tilley's party and squeezed two shots from a pistol, then ducked down again.

Caddie's blur of an impression told her that the man was not Tilley. Why was someone other than the boatswain shooting?

The men sheltering in and behind the *Miss Faye IX* let loose a barrage of fire directed toward Tilley's party. The workboat's floodlights came on, throwing the scene into bright relief.

"Now." Caddie swung around the boulder that had shielded her and hopped to the next rock, holding her pistol before her.

One of the smugglers, crouching between their boat's bow and a black rock, jerked around and stared toward them.

Caddie recognized the large, bearded figure of Spruce Waller. His long gun came up, pointing at her men, and Caddie let off a round in his general direction, not pausing long enough to get a good aim.

The man flattened himself behind the hull of the boat.

All around her, pistols discharged. She reached a fairly flat stretch of rocks and ran forward, brandishing her weapon. To her left, her peripheral vision caught the shadows of two men leaping up from Tilley's position and running forward.

The man in the smugglers' boat went down. Spruce Waller rose on his knees and fired, then jerked back onto the ground, his weapon flying to one side.

McQuillan tackled the third man on the jagged rocks, and two others ran to assist him.

Caddie hastily collected their adversaries' weapons while her men secured the prisoners. "How bad is the wounded man?" she asked Torres.

"Petty Officer Lyle!"

She whirled toward the voice.

One of Tilley's men waved frantically. "The bo'sun's hit!"

fourteen

Aven's stomach churned as he waited for his orders.

The *Milroy* passed the much larger *Wintergreen* and drove steadily toward the small workboat near the rocky island in the bay. The radio chatter had lessened and all but stopped during the last few minutes. The rain seemed to let up, but a drizzle still dampened everything, and the cold wind kept working conditions uncomfortable.

His men waited with him on the dark deck, staring toward their destination—a pile of black rocks with a constant warning buoy. The temporary addition of small boats looked innocent from this distance.

A sudden glare of floodlights illuminated the island, and with binoculars, Aven could see figures moving about. The *Milroy*'s engine and the wind drowned any sound from the tableau, but from this side, it looked like a miniature battle. Had the *Wintergreen*'s crew forced a confrontation with the drug smugglers?

At last his radio came to life again.

A man's voice drawled in an almost bored tone, "*Wintergreen*, this is *Wintergreen 2*. We have two casualties needing medical assistance. One of them is a prisoner. Total three prisoners requiring transport. Request permission to transfer prisoners and our wounded to the *Wintergreen*. Over."

Captain Raven of the *Wintergreen* replied, "Negative, *Wintergreen 2*. Law enforcement cutter *Milroy* approaching. Hand prisoners over to them unless critical medical care is needed. Transport our wounded personnel to *Wintergreen*."

Aven's adrenaline surged. One of the *Wintergreen*'s crew

was wounded, as well as one of the prisoners. Was Caddie safe?

&

Caddie hurried with Seaman Jackson to the place where Tilley and his two men had crouched behind the rocks.

Tilley lay on his side, both hands clamped to his thigh.

"They hit him right away," Jackson said.

Caddie frowned at him. "Why didn't you report it?"

"He didn't want them to know they'd got him. They might have rushed us. And he knew you were on the way."

She climbed over a rounded rock and knelt at the boatswain's side. "Tilley, how you doing?"

Pain flickered across his taut features. "Not so good. It's bleeding a lot."

"We'll get you out of here. I've got one of my men calling it in. We'll transport you immediately to the *Wintergreen*." She noted the position of the wound. To her relief, the entrance wound was on the outside of his thigh. Probably it hadn't severed the femoral artery. "Do you think the bullet hit the bone?"

"Not sure. Maybe not. All I know is it hurts."

"Let me put some pressure on it, if you can stand it. We'll put you in the Zodiac and get you out to the ship."

Engine noises nearly drowned her words and obscured the now-busy radio traffic. She turned to look down the bay and saw a ship approaching. Not the *Wintergreen*, but a patrol boat half as big. Reinforcements. She grinned. A law enforcement cutter. No doubt the crew was ready to land, armed to the teeth. She squeezed Tilley's leg at the point of the wound. He groaned but didn't protest. *That's good,* she thought. Knowing him, if it were broken, he'd be cussing a blue streak.

Gavin came to her side. "McQuillan has gone to help Morrison beach the Zodiac."

Tilley said between his clenched teeth, "Did you search that boat yet?"

"Not yet." Caddie looked up at McQuillan. "Can you take over here? Pressure on the wound until we get him to the hospital corpsman."

She let the seaman take her place and rose. Three of her men had brought the prisoners together on the rocks facing the *Wintergreen 1*.

"Libby," she called. "Come with me."

She and the seaman approached the damaged boat.

Caddie climbed into the *Miss Faye IX* and quickly made sure no one else was aboard. The cabin seemed warm and quiet, since the wind no longer howled about her. When she saw the sophisticated radio equipment, she pursed her lips, but they were too chapped to whistle. Clay Waller knew where to put his money.

"Lyle."

She turned toward Libby's voice.

"Take a look in these lockers."

She walked to his side and peered into the cupboard he'd opened. A crate full of plastic bags lay inside. Each bag bulged with a white powder.

"I'm betting it's cocaine," Libby said.

They quickly opened more lockers. Caddie had never seen so much contraband. She put in a call on her radio.

"*Wintergreen*, this is *Wintergreen 2*. We have a cargo on the hostiles' vessel that appears to be narcotics."

"*Wintergreen 2*, I copy," came her captain's voice. "Turn all evidence over to the petty officer now landing from the *Milroy*."

Caddie jerked her head up and stared toward the cutter now anchored just beyond the workboat Tilley had commanded. She smiled for the first time all evening. Aven had arrived with the cavalry.

❧

Mark came directly to the *Miss Faye IX.* "Lyle!" He grinned at her. "Looks like you got the job done, hey?"

"I think so. Captain Raven says to turn this pile of contraband over to you." She shined her flashlight on a part of the drug stash.

"Happy to accept." Mark glanced around then leaned toward her. "Aven was worried sick about you. Better show your face outside."

She felt her face flush. When she left the cabin, Libby was waiting to give her a hand as she climbed over the gunwale and dropped to the rocks below. They scrambled over the boulders toward the *Milroy*'s landing party.

Aven had his back to her as he helped lift Tilley into the Zodiac manned by Seamen Morrison and McQuillan. As soon as he was settled, Tilley growled, "Let's move. Somebody radio the *Wintergreen* and tell them."

"Got it," Aven called and shoved the Zodiac off the rocks. He turned, reaching for his radio. As he spotted Caddie, his face broke into a huge smile. "This is *Milroy 1*," he said into the transmitter. "Inform *Wintergreen* her boatswain is being transported in *Wintergreen 2*, who requests permission to come alongside."

He took two long strides to reach Caddie. They stood for a moment in the cold mist, appraising each other.

What was he thinking? If the men weren't here, would he light into her for endangering herself? Would he take Tilley's tack and berate her for wanting to do "a man's job"?

Aven nodded slowly. "Looks to me as though you did a good job, Petty Officer."

❧

Three weeks later, Caddie got her lunch tray in the mess hall and sat down with Lindsey.

"What's up?" Lindsey asked, lowering her voice so that it

reached Caddie beneath the level of the chatter surrounding them. "You've been smiley-eyed all morning. Did you get a message from Holland?"

Caddie chuckled. "I don't know anyone in Holland."

"Very funny. You know who I mean."

"Did you realize that when we dock it will be less than a week until Thanksgiving?"

"No," Lindsey said, "I didn't know that. But I guess you don't want to talk about whatever it is that's—"

She stopped talking, and the lunchtime buzz dropped away as suddenly. Caddie looked toward the hatch. Captain Raven had just entered. He walked to the middle of the room.

"At ease, everyone. I have an announcement—the kind I like making in person." His gaze darted about the room, lingering for a moment on Caddie and Lindsey. "It's my pleasure to tell you that BM3 Lyle is now BM2 Lyle. Congratulations, Second Class Bo'sun's Mate."

Caddie nodded, blushing, as the twenty men present, along with Lindsey and Vera Hotchkiss, began clapping and cheering.

"Thanks!" Caddie waved and concentrated on her food.

"I'm also pleased to report that Bo'sun Tilley is doing well. However, he's got several weeks of rehab ahead, and he's decided to take retirement. He won't be returning to the *Wintergreen*."

A surprised murmur rippled over the room.

"Carry on," the captain said. He smiled at Caddie and left the compartment.

"That's great about your promotion!" Lindsey grinned at her, still clapping. "So that's what made you so happy."

"Thank you. I just. . ." Caddie picked up her knife and attacked the chicken leg on her plate.

"Have you sent a message to your mom? She'll be so proud of you."

Caddie shook her head. "Not yet."

"Why not?"

"No time. I just found out this morning." A tear popped over Caddie's eyelid and trickled down her cheek. She swiped it quickly away with her napkin.

"Oh, wait a minute," Lindsey said, tilting her head to one side. "You're thinking of your dad, aren't you?"

"Maybe. I don't know."

"Sure you are. Wishing he could share this moment with you."

Caddie wagged her head back and forth. "There have been a lot of moments he hasn't been there to share with me." *Some even before he died,* she thought.

"Yeah, but. . ." Lindsey raised her hands, palms out. "Okay, I'll be quiet. Sorry. But it would be nice if you could get home for Thanksgiving."

"I'll settle for Christmas," Caddie said.

"Yeah, it's great that they've timed our next deployment so that most of us will be able to take leave at Christmas. I've decided to spend it with my mom. Maybe not the whole time, but a few days anyway."

"That's wonderful."

Lindsey smiled brightly. "Hey, does Aven— Oops, sorry."

Caddie chuckled. "I don't know what his plans are yet or what his December schedule looks like. He got home for a week right after our run-in with the *Miss Faye IX*. I was glad he had the chance and went to Wasilla."

"If he's in Kodiak next week, maybe you can spend Thanksgiving together."

"Maybe, but I'm not planning on it."

Lindsey nodded. "Same as always, where men are concerned, huh? We can't count on them being there."

❧

Aven stood on the deck of the moored *Milroy*, watching the harbor.

"Hey, Holland," Mark shouted. "You ready to go home?"

"No, go along without me."

Mark laughed. "I heard the *Wintergreen* will be here within the hour. Guess we won't see you tonight."

Aven grinned. "If she needs to stay on board or is too tired to eat out, I'll drag myself over to your place."

"Hey, did you hear they're holding the Waller brothers in Anchorage until their trial?"

"No," Aven said. "I'm glad they didn't let them out on bail. Is Spruce still in the hospital?"

"I don't know. I just heard from the skipper that all three of the smugglers were denied bail." Mark swung down the metal stairway onto the dock and headed off whistling.

This was silly. Even when the ship came in, it would be awhile before she could leave. Maybe long enough to run to the florist? Or should he save the money toward a trip to Wasilla together, or even toward extra for his family this month?

In the end, he stuck it out and was on the dock waiting when the *Wintergreen* put in. At four o'clock the sun was nearly down, but seeing Caddie's face when she spotted him was worth the nearly three hours he had whiled away. When she came off the ship, he didn't care if all the sailors in the Seventeenth District saw. She flipped the hood of her parka back, dropped her sea bag, and ran toward him. He pulled her into his arms and held her right there on the dock.

"Welcome back," he whispered near her ear. He tossed her bag into the back of his pickup and drove her home.

All the way, she smiled and told him about things she'd seen since their brief meeting on the rocky island where she'd caught the smugglers. He stopped at the post office, and she dashed inside, returning with a handful of mail.

When they reached her apartment, she jumped down from the truck. "Want to come in?"

"Uh. . .what do you think? Want some time to get

settled? I can come back in a while. I thought maybe we'd eat out tonight?"

"Great. Give me an hour?"

He went away for the time stipulated and wound up hanging out with Mark and Jo-Lynn. He took their good-natured teasing but turned down Jo-Lynn's offer of a snack.

At last he was back on Caddie's doorstep. There had to be a way to spend more than an evening together every few weeks.

Her blue eyes lit up when she opened the door. She pulled him inside, and he hugged her again. Her draped green shirt was soft and very unmilitary, and her blond hair lay in shimmery waves about her shoulders.

"You look great."

"Thanks. Aven, I sold the article."

"Which one?" He slid his hand over her satiny hair.

"The one about Lindsey. Remember, I told you about it. And the magazine wants more profiles. So maybe I can do the one we talked about—on your sister."

"That'd be great." He let her slip out of his arms to get her coat and purse. "Say, have you got Christmas leave?"

"Yes. Thirty days. Have you?"

He nodded. "Are you going home?"

"I thought I would." She eyed him uncertainly.

"You should," he said, "but what about. . .I don't suppose you could come back for the last week? Fly into Anchorage?"

Her heart-stopping smile spread over her face. "I'd love to. And I can see Robyn work her dogs then."

"And take pictures," he added.

"If your family doesn't mind. . ."

"They're begging me to get you there."

"I'd love to."

She flowed back into his embrace, and he stooped to kiss her. Perfect.

epilogue

Caddie and her uncle waited on the bridge of the *Milroy*. Watching out the window, they saw Jo-Lynn and Lindsey emerge onto the main deck below. Aven, who now served as boatswain of the cutter, stood on the main deck below, with their pastor, Mark Phifer, and Lieutenant Greer. The petty officer who had volunteered to run the sound system today started the wedding march, and Caddie smiled up at her father's younger brother.

"Come on, Uncle Jack. Looks like it's our turn."

"Okay, honey. Be careful."

She clung to his hand on the ladder as they went cautiously down to the deck. Once on stable footing, they walked slowly in time to the music, toward where the minister stood. Mark and Jo-Lynn's baby let out a whimper, and Dee Morrison, who had volunteered to hold him during the ceremony, bounced the infant gently and shushed him.

The brilliant early July sun smiled down on the moored cutter. A gentle breeze fluttered Caddie's veil and the long skirt of her gown. She picked out her mom, smiling at her through tears, and Mira and Jordan grinning from ear to ear. The only one missing from her family was Dad. She'd cried a little last night, when Uncle Jack had arrived looking so much like her father. Now she was able to smile at them without weeping.

"Isn't this kind of weird?" Jordan had asked her last night. "You and Aven being married and still being on different ships, I mean."

"It may be hard for a while, but we'll manage," Caddie had assured him.

Aven's mother, sister, and grandfather stood on the other side, smiling as well, but her focus came back to Aven.

He and his two groomsmen stood at attention in their dress uniforms, but Caddie had opted for traditional gowns for herself and her bridesmaids. Lindsey had threatened to throttle Caddie if she had to wear her uniform instead of a pretty dress, and Jo-Lynn had pointed out that she was a civilian, anyway, and they all ought to be dressed in similar styles.

Aven's dark eyes shone as Caddie and Uncle Jack approached.

When handing her over to Aven, Uncle Jack leaned over and kissed her on the cheek. "Bless you," he whispered, and pressed her hand before going to stand with Mom.

Mira popped off a flash picture with Caddie's camera.

Caddie looked up at Aven and read his lips as he mouthed, "Love you."

She couldn't speak, her heart was so full, but she gave his hand a squeeze as they turned to face the pastor.

After his welcome to their families and friends, the pastor said, "Folks, we're gathered here in a somewhat unusual venue to witness the union of two people who've chosen careers full of adventure, and yes, sometimes danger. These young people have pledged to serve the United States of America, and as the motto of the Coast Guard says, to be 'always ready' when they're needed. Well, I'm here to tell you all that I've spent several hours talking to Aven and Caddie, and I can assure you, they're ready for this."

The people chuckled, and Caddie sneaked another look at Aven. His energy flowed to her through their clasped hands, and her anticipation mounted.

She would be a petty officer for another year at least, but after that, who knew? Only the Lord. Whatever He brought her way, she would be ready. And today, she would begin her new life as Aven's wife.

A Letter To Our Readers

Dear Reader:

In order that we might better contribute to your reading enjoyment, we would appreciate your taking a few minutes to respond to the following questions. We welcome your comments and read each form and letter we receive. When completed, please return to the following:

Fiction Editor
Heartsong Presents
PO Box 719
Uhrichsville, Ohio 44683

1. Did you enjoy reading *Always Ready* by Susan Page Davis?
   ☐ Very much! I would like to see more books by this author!
   ☐ Moderately. I would have enjoyed it more if

   _____

   _____

   _____

2. Are you a member of **Heartsong Presents**? ☐ Yes ☐ No
   If no, where did you purchase this book? _____

   _____

3. How would you rate, on a scale from 1 (poor) to 5 (superior), the cover design? _____

4. On a scale from 1 (poor) to 10 (superior), please rate the following elements.

   ____ Heroine   ____ Plot
   ____ Hero   ____ Inspirational theme
   ____ Setting   ____ Secondary characters

5. These characters were special because? _____
   _____
   _____

6. How has this book inspired your life? _____
   _____
   _____

7. What settings would you like to see covered in future
   Heartsong Presents books? _____
   _____
   _____

8. What are some inspirational themes you would like to see
   treated in future books? _____
   _____
   _____

9. Would you be interested in reading other **Heartsong
   Presents** titles? ❏ Yes ❏ No

10. Please check your age range:
    ❏ Under 18   ❏ 18-24
    ❏ 25-34   ❏ 35-45
    ❏ 46-55   ❏ Over 55

Name_____

Occupation _____

Address _____

City, State, Zip_____

LOVE IS A BATTLEFIELD

Left at the altar, her old job filled by someone else, all Kristy O'Neal wants is for life to return to normal. But working as a seasonal park ranger at Shiloh National Military Park alongside Ace Kennedy, the man who stole her job, may be more than Kristy can handle—especially when she realizes she's falling for him. But Kristy doesn't believe in true love anymore. With the history of her beloved park and his ancestors in his arsenal, Ace begins the battle to prove to Kristy that true love does exist. . .before he loses her forever.

Contemporary, paperback, 320 pages, 5¾6" x 8"

_____

Presents

Great Inspirational Romance at a Great Price!

Heartsong Presents books are inspirational romances in
contemporary and historical settings, designed to give you an
enjoyable, spirit-lifting reading experience. You can choose
wonderfully written titles from some of today's best authors like
Wanda E. Brunstetter, Mary Connealy, Susan Page Davis,
Cathy Marie Hake, Joyce Livingston, and many others.

When ordering quantities less than twelve, above titles are $2.97 each.
Not all titles may be available at time of order.